COLT & BIG THUNDER

A Western Novel

BY T. L. Sheldon

BIG THUNDER PUBLISHING

Published by:
Big Thunder Publishing,

P.O. Box 82836,
San Diego, CA 92138

www.bigthunder.org

Cover Artist: Norma de Flon

Cover and Interior Design by Scribe Freelance
www.scribefreelance.com

ISBN: 978-0-9821867-3-2
LC Control Number: 2010927885
Printed in the United States of America

This book is dedicated to the Memory of

ARVO OJALA

*who taught me the six-gun tricks described in this book
(even though I can't do them).*

*(Arvo was the outlaw opposite Matt Dillon at the beginning of every episode
of* Gunsmoke, *and who taught many Hollywood gunslingers the art of quick
draw. He patented the holsters used by many a Star including Richard Boone's
in* Have Gun Will Travel. *The Arvo rigs the author owns were worn by Ricky
Nelson in* Rio Bravo, *Robert Fuller in* Lawmen *and two remakes of
Paladin's rig and others.)*

CHAPTER ONE

FOUR TO THE DEVIL

When Big Thunder hit the quicksand his rider grabbed the Winchester saddle ring carbine with his right hand and rolled left off the horse landing flat on his back on the unstable river bed. The horse's stomach had caught the initial impact of the sand and it was Thunder's girth that kept them afloat for a few seconds. The rider's boots were wet, and if you can call that good luck, it was fortunate that was all, because had the quicksand been less dense they both would have sunk over their heads on impact into the mush.

At full gallop when they hit the deceptive hazard the air whistled out of Thunder's lungs like a shrill wind. Winston still held the reins in his left hand and he rolled back towards the bank of what had looked to be a dry wash. He kept his grip on the reins but he did not pull on the horse. When he was able to stand up on the bank he watched the horse take deep breathes of air to fill his stomach and lungs as he continued his forward heaves until like a rocking horse in slow motion he heaved and floated himself out of the sandy muck. Thunder stood up as though relieved he had dodged a worse fate. He shook himself in a violent vibrating shiver throwing wet sand everywhere, and then just stood bewildered looking at his pal. The next thing Winston heard was, "Whiiiizzzzzzz, plop."

The bullet landed in the wet sand near them. They were in the open. There was no protection. Winston dropped his rifle, threw one arm around Thunder's neck, and with the other arm he grabbed the horse around the nose. Then he turned Thunder's head hard as he pushed the horse off balance. They both crashed down against the dry part of the sandy river bank. Thunder knew to stay down but Winston hobbled his front feet with the reins anyway. He did not want his horse shot.

Winston left Thunder's side and grabbed the rifle. He couldn't tell from which direction the bullet had come because the plop of quicksand had risen straight upwards. He twirled around but still saw no one. That was strange, he thought, considering the three horsemen who had been chasing him hadn't seemed that far away. Then he saw them; three men on paints riding hard towards him from the distant trees.

"Wish I had some religion," he whispered to himself, "but I guess apostles Winchester and Colt here will have to do for now. Let's see if Uncle Samuel was right about his makin' us equal." Then he knelt on his left knee, unhitched the loop that held his Colt .45 in the right holster, leaving the left pistol holstered and secure, and then he raised the rifle to his shoulder.

Three bullets fell in front of him.

"You guys shoot good on the run," he complimented his adversaries. Then he let fly a .44/75 slug from his rifle that felled the middle rider. Two more shots came at him, one grazing his knee and the other clipped his hat. He levered another round in the chamber and shot quickly. Too quickly, because he had only hit the left rider's hat which blew off behind him. "Breathe slowly, now," he scolded himself, "or you won't be breathin' at all."

He took careful aim, but noticed that his care was only allowing both riders to get too close too quickly. He squeezed off another round that seemed to hit the left rider in the right shoulder causing him to pull too hard on his right rein and veer off from the man's target; him. The rider to his right snapped off two quick successive shots from his sidearm. One of them slapped hard the side of Winston's holster, spinning him to the right. He dropped the Winchester.

There is no collection of thoughts in fights. One either reacts from experience to the adversary, or one gets dead. Winston spun around and was nearly trampled by the rider's horse but followed the motion 'til he was full circle. Instinctively he drew and cocked his sidearm and pointed it at the rider's back and pulled the trigger. The .45 caliber slug slammed into the man's shoulder, causing him to fall from his horse.

Ire and adrenaline rush madness pushed Winston towards the final kill of his would be assassin. He had no clue why these men wanted him dead, and he didn't care. He just wanted to finish what they had started. The man staggered up to his feet and when he turned towards the oncoming Winston, he raised his hands in submission. The men were no more than twenty feet apart by now.

"Where's your gun, you coward. Don't give up now, come on, try to kill me," Winston screamed.

"I can…..can't," the man choked, "I'm hit bad. Don't kill me, please don't kill me," he pleaded.

Winston did not lower his gun. It was cocked and the ambusher saw him moving his trigger finger. Sweat was pouring from under the man's hat, wetting his dusty face to a muddy mess. There was a moment of complete silence between the men. The adrenaline from both men seemed to deafen them both to the outside world. Then the pounding of hooves from the rider that had veered off came from behind Winston. Winston first heard dull thudding until his animal awareness heightened his hearing to tell him what was coming.

He turned and saw the man and horse intending to run him down. The hole the .45-75 slug had made in the man's shoulder was gushing so much blood that mixed with the rising dust from the galloping hooves it caked a deep red mud that covered both man and horse as the beast spat dusty fire-like breath and the sun reflected blazing hot crazed eyes of this *Devil's* steed. All together this gave Winston the impression that a demon intended to trample him to hell.

Winston reacted. He shot the horse between the eyes.

The paint dropped in a heap not two feet from where Winston stood. The rider's body hurled sideways off the horse. He hit the hard pan head first, bending his neck under his body against the ground making a loud, dull cracking sound. The fallen rider's head stayed unnaturally bent under his body, which twitched in death.

Winston turned quickly to deal with whatever threat may still be coming from the other man who was now behind him. His Colt .45 was cocked again and ready to kill once more, but Winston hesitated. The man was just standing like a rag doll before him. Winston wanted to pull the trigger but he just couldn't do it.

"I never see'd no man shoot a horse before, least not a healthy one," the assassin gasped, "but, I guess ya had ta."

"Never had to before. Rather have shot you than that horse," Winston growled. "Why were you after me?"

"We thought you were headed to the Double M. You'd have..." he faded, then the man staggered towards Winston and fell in a thud at his feet. Winston uncocked the revolver and holstered it. He felt his heart beating hard under his black shirt. He opened the two top buttons, pulled the black cotton scarf from his neck and wiped his brow. Then it struck him; Big Thunder.

Winston looked to where he had left his horse. He heard a nagging whinny and saw his horse struggling impatiently but in vain to get up. The look on the horse's face sent a streak of guilt through Winston's loyal soul. He knew he had done the right thing by hobbling the horse to the ground, but he also knew that he had deprived Big Thunder from being Big Thunder, who was always a part of the action. Winston untied Thunder who rose up, shook off the dust and snorted muddy snot in Winston's face.

"Guess I deserved that, boy," he apologized, wiping the muck from his forehead.

Thunder nuzzled him and he held the horse's head in his arms with his face against the steed's cheek, and said, "Dame un beso." Thunder raised his upper lip and pressed it against Winston's face, who stroked his pal's nose and responded, "Yo te amo, hermano."

When he opened his eyes Winston saw a group of a half dozen or so riders trotting towards them. "Not more of 'em, I hope," he murmured.

Winston mounted Thunder and rode to where his rifle was laying in the dust. He reached down, retrieved the rifle and placed it in its tooled leather scabbard tied to his saddle. He took a squinted look at the oncoming riders and noticed there was a buggy in the midst of the group. He removed the rifle from the scabbard and decided to stay mounted so as to see who was coming and why; or maybe to make another run for it.

Winston laid the rifle across his lap and pulled the Colt Single Action

Army from the holster and quickly ejected the three spent rounds. He deftly pulled three fresh rounds from this gunbelt and reloaded. With a quick flip he spun the pistol into its home base. He unhooked the loop from the holster holding his left pistol, drew it, flipped open the loading gate with the hammer half cocked then spun it to check that all six bullets were at ready. They were, so he closed it up. Then he drew the right pistol. Balancing both factory nickel and engraved 4-3/4 inch barreled Colt .45's he spun them twice until they easily circled back into their respective holsters. On their way in they gleamed in the sun like a message mirror, and he hoped the oncoming riders saw that. He always advised carrying a nickel plated gun because day or night the flash of the finish told any potential attacker to beware, that a gun was in hand.

He picked up the Winchester, cocked a fresh round in the chamber, then ready in his right hand, and a single action Colt ready at his left, he watched the posse slowly move in his direction.

The mounted riders stopped about a hundred yards from where Winston stood. The buggy kept coming and as it neared Winston could see the driver was a woman. She pulled up to a respectful territorial distance and stopped. He couldn't yet make out her face in the shade of the surrey top, but he did see she had long hair flowing all over her shoulders.

"Looks like you solved our problem for us," she yelled. "Mind if I come a little closer."

"Maybe when I get to know ya better," Winston answered, raising the Winchester up to lean the barrel on his shoulder.

"Don't blame you for the caution," she agreed, "I'm Marilyn Montgomery. This is my spread; MM brand, the Double M ranch. Those three stole my horses." She looked around for a moment. She spotted two horses standing not far away. "Where's the third horse?" she asked.

Winston side passed Thunder away from blocking her view. Behind them was the body of the dead paint and the dead man. She dismounted her buggy. Winston took a deep breath when he saw her left profile. She was beautiful. Flaming red hair flowed everywhere and even covering the right side of her face. She had ghostly light blue eyes that stared right past him to where her horse lay. She looked to be pretty tall as she strode past him not more than 10 feet away. She wore no hat and appeared to wear no gun. Her jeans were tight on her body and tucked into her boots. Her red shirt that amply bulged in front was tucked inside the thin waistline. The only fancy thing she wore were a pair of boots that were red with rearing white and black paint horses tooled on both sides of the boot necks. She stood over her fallen horse and a tear rolled down her cheek.

"One of the meanest stallions I've ever known," she murmured, "but the best stud of the breed."

"Sorry, ma'am," he apologized sheepishly, finally realizing the act of killing the horse was a very unpleasant thing for him, too. "Had no choice."

"There's always a choice, mister! Who the hell did you say you are?" she demanded.

"Didn't say."

"Then *say* now," she demanded more forcefully this time.

"Colt. Winston Colt," he replied with pride.

"That's rich," she said snidely, "using that famous name when you're nothing but a horse killer."

"It's my family name," he defended. "And I'm not sorry, lady. It was me or the horse. He came right at me with all 1200 pounds or so; mouth open and hooves ready to cut me to pieces. I know it wasn't his choice, and for that I'm truly sorry for the horse. But, you gotta…"

"I don't *gotta*," she scolded, "anything. But…I get the picture." She walked over and kicked the fallen man near the horse and screamed at him, "You had to be some rider to get on Ol' Danger's back and make him do the things you made him do. And I hate you for that!" Then she walked off a few yards and turned her back away from Winston. He let her alone and just stood and waited for the next tirade. She finally turned towards Winston and said, "Guess I'll just round up the two mares and go home,"

Winston shrugged. The lady walked past him and mounted her buggy. Her red hair now seemed to be a head of flames, and it all still covered the right side of her face. She climbed in under the surrey top and the shade again darkened her face.

"I had offered a reward for the return of the three horses. $300 a head. You earned two-thirds of it. You can collect back at my place," she spat at Winston.

"I'm used to 'Dead or Alive' rewards," he shot back, realizing at once it was a bad joke. He cringed as Marilyn turned the buggy around, who was now smiling, but Winston couldn't see that part.

"We'll send someone out to clean up this mess," she said, matter of factly. Then she turned the buggy to go. "I was gonna sell you no 'count mean devil horse anyway," she said to herself, "the girls were getting' tired of your biting attitude." Then she whipped the reins a bit and smooched the air to signal the horse to pull her buggy faster towards the group of horses.

"Marilyn Montgomery," Winston whispered to himself as he turned to look at Thunder. "Recognize that name ol' boy?" he asked the horse. Thunder lowered his head and nudged his pal. "Me neither," he agreed.

CHAPTER TWO
DOUBLE M'S

The main house of Marilyn Montgomery's MM ranch was large by most standards at a working horse and cattle ranch in the Colorado foothills under the looming Rocky Mountains. She took it all in as she rocked in a bent wood chair on the large front porch overlooking the valley with a pitcher of snow chilled lemonade on the table. Her foreman was there with her.

"Miss Marilyn," the foreman broke silence as he handed her a glass of lemonade, "you had quite a day."

"Rocky, how can three men who work for you for so long, take your property and think its okay?" she asked.

"Don't know. Greed I guess. Men get bored, stupid, don't think straight sometimes out here. What about the puncher what caught 'em?" he prodded.

"Says his name is Winston Colt. I offered him $600 reward. He'll probably be around to collect. "

"I thought the reward was $900, Miss M."

"He shot one of the horses."

"Gotta be a story there somewhere," he ended, knowing he'd hear about it some other time. "I know that name, though."

"From where?" she feigned boredom.

"All the usual places. Dodge, Abilene, Denver, Texas, Tombstone, you know."

"No, I don't know."

"He's a relative or somethin' to Samuel Colt, is what I recall. He works for his family's company and does some peacekeepin' on the side and sometimes helps bring in the bad guys."

"Low life bounty hunter. It figures. And how do you know all that?"

she doubted.

"I haven't always been a ranch hand, ya know," he reminded.

"Yeah, daddy told me. Texas Rangers, U.S. Marshal, all around top gun. I remember. Pretty colorful past, as I recall. No offense."

"We can vouch for the color part, but I don't know about *colorful*," he chuckled. "But I did run into Mr. Winston Colt on one occasion, but I doubt he'll remember."

"Really," she got interested, sitting up straighter in her chair.

"Remember I went to Denver in '79. We was all at a U.S. Marshals meeting for the territorial divisions by the gov'ment. Had a shooting exhibition and competition. Winston won in both repeating rifles and six-guns. But, he won't remember me."

"Whatever he is, he's a real looker," she said half daydreaming.

"What's that?" Rocky leaned closer to hear.

"Look, I bet that's him coming up the road," she answered.

"Interesting gear he has. I wonder if he still has the rifle he won?"

"What's it look like?"

"Winchester Model '73 one of one thousand. Solid brass receiver engraved with buffalo and eagles."

"He still has it," she confirmed. "That wide brimmed straw hat with the flat crown he wears is odd in these parts."

"He rides a *Spanish* horse, I think. Big white monster, so the hat goes with that style of riding," he commented, looking up at the looming horse and rider that was arriving in front of them.

Winston Colt passed by two large tree trunk sized pine posts still with the bark on. They were holding up an equally large notched log beam that stretched ten yards across the road and was emblazoned with three foot high bolted on heavy steel letters that identified the brand and name of the ranch; MM.

As he passed under the brand, Winston espied a large two story log built house that was about a quarter mile away. It was framed by the Rocky Mountains which were lightly dusted with the first fall snows. The mountains were forested with the still yellowed stands of aspen trees surrounded by huge pines wending in ages old patterns of harmony and territorial patchworks that probably changed back and forth over the eons. He rode slowly to admire the breathtaking beauty until he arrived right up to the porch. He let Thunder drop his head to take a lick or two from the water trough.

"Howdy, Miss Montgomery," Winston politely greeted.

"You can call me Marilyn, since you don't work for me," she offered.

He lifted his hat, revealing silky, wavy, gleaming brown hair.

She rocked back and viewed this stranger fully this time. He seemed strong, muscled, as the material of his shirt clung over the arms and shoulders and seemed to stretch when he moved. His jeans were close fitted, like the English riders and tucked into his tall black boots that were spurred with the old heavy Mexican silver. She hadn't noticed before the two guns hanging from the gleaming black leather holsters and as he sat astride his stallion she saw that each holster had a medallion on it of a rearing horse made from silver with an eye that appeared to be turquoise. She knew the Colt firearms symbol and this more or less validated Rocky's explanation. His wide brimmed straw plantation hat was darkened at where the crown met the brim from what appeared to be years of sweat and dust, and there was a horsehair band that looked to have been made from the white and grey strands from his horse's mane and tail. It was a lot to take in all at once, she thought, but the view pleased her.

"You must be thirsty after all your hard work," she offered, "so get off that big boy and have a lemonade, and Rocky here will get your money."

"Kinda used ta givin' orders aren't you?" Winston challenged.

Marilyn stood up, did a curtsy and in a southern belle's voice said, "Well, suh, would you kindlay join us for a refreshment?"

Winston dismounted, grabbed his Peruvian style straw hat which he had had custom made by the world's best hat makers in Ecuador, then by its broad brim he waved it across his body as he bowed and said, "Why, thank ya, ma'am, yor courtesy and hospitalatee shore do seem most gen-u-wine and is most appreciated by this gentle man."

"Oh, now my dea' suh, a gentleman, nay, a *gentle man*, would neva' kill a *lady's* horse, now would he?"

"*Ladies* don't have horses that would kill a man," he retorted, not to be out-challenged.

"We've met," Rocky interrupted so the bantering wouldn't turn into a feud.

Winston strode up onto the porch. His thick iron Mexican spurs with silver engraving jingled as he climbed each stair. He reached out his right hand. He felt the grip of a man whose hands could crush a milk bottle. "I'd never forget a grip like that," Winston remembered. "We met a few years ago at the U.S. Marshals get together. Men like you are hard to forget. Your type of lawman is rare."

"I didn't think you'd remember, son. But, there aren't many of my kind trusted to do that job. I was lucky."

"I remember the handshake and the smile, but the name escapes me, sir," he apologized.

"Rocky Mountain," the big man proudly smiled, as he rose up to his fully more than six foot height and puffed his barrel chest 'til it seemed his braces would pop off his pants.

"And from what I remember, it wasn't luck, you bein' a U.S.Marshal. I saw you win the single shot big bore rifle competition with that .50 caliber buffalo gun. You still shoot that good?" Winston asked.

"Kinda," Rocky responded modestly. "But it was actually a .69 caliber smoothbore."

"He's probably better now," Marilyn chimed in. "Give him his money, please, Rocky," she ordered as though she resented having to part with it to Winston.

Rocky handed the money to Winston, who looked at the six one hundred dollar gold pieces in his hand. Then he dropped them all into his front pocket. He sat down in the rocker next to Marilyn, grabbed a cold glass and emptied the lemonade into his parched throat and placed the glass back on the table. She lifted the pitcher and promptly filled it again for him. He nodded appreciation, picked up the glass, drank about a third of it, then held the cold glass against his face. "I needed that. Thank you kindly," he said.

Marilyn was staring at him. He smiled and his light green eyes stared

15

right back into her stream deep blue eyes. The moment froze for both of them. It wasn't a challenging look from either of them. Sometimes it happens that a man and a woman can see past each other's eyes on such an encounter and they feel at peace. This was not one of those occasions. Winston saw fire and unease. Marilyn felt fear of her feelings.

Winston noticed that her long red hair never seemed to leave the right side of her face. It had always covered and shaded that side of her face. She seemed to be hiding something, but he was not about to inquire what. The moment of locked eyes seemed longer than it really was, but their mutual appraisal amused Rocky.

"So," Rocky began, "what brings you to this part of the world?"

"Well," Winston awoke, "I'm headed for the gunsmith in Sage Brush Springs to deliver a gun from our custom department. That's what I thought those three desperados were after, to tell the truth."

"Fancy pistol, no doubt," Rocky prodded.

"Very," Winston said, raising his eyebrows. "Peacemaker Colt .44's. Cased set. Long barrels, raised eagles on mastodon ivory grips, factory engraved nickel frames with blue barrels and two sets of cylinders. Pretty unique pieces. I've only seen the purchase order, so I'm looking forward to actually seeing them."

"Who are they for?" Marilyn asked.

"Don't really know," Winston said as he finished a sip of lemonade. "These kind of orders are mostly gifts. Must be an engraving on the backstraps, but I've not opened the case to see."

"The gunsmith in town is Paddy McIrish," Rocky informed, "and he's not only good at fixin' guns, he's better usin' 'em."

"I don't know of him," Winston said, "but the order was prepaid including my personal delivery."

"Oh, then you've done really well for yourself on this trip," Marilyn chided.

Rocky and Winston locked eyes and both rolled them at the same time. There was no need for a verbal response.

"Well, guess I've worn out my welcome," Winston offered, as he stood up and set his hat.

"Oh, not at all," Marilyn entreated, "I'd like you to stay the night and for dinner to thank you for your efforts today, and…."

Winston saw some remorse in her ever challenging eyes. Her lips were quivering with a selfish regret that she wasn't going to get what she wanted this time, and Winston obliged that fact with, "Not this time, ma'am. But, I'll take a rain check if I have the time."

As the woman's blue eyes seemed to turn to red, Rocky could not restrain a huge spontaneous laugh. In total exasperation, Marilyn twirled like a Spanish flamenco dancer. Her red and white pleated skirt twirled wildly and her heels clicked on the porch boards as though she was dancing the hot, raging challenge of that passionate dance. But it wasn't passion at all, and both men knew it. When she stormed into the house, they both laughed loudly at the spectacle.

"I think she likes you," Rocky offered with a wink.

"You may be right, but would you please take this knife out of my chest," Winston joked.

Winston stepped down off the porch as Rocky placed his big hand on the man's shoulder. Winston felt the warmth of the gesture and knew he had at least one friend in this place. As he turned to face the big man, the hand from his shoulder dropped and found his own right hand in a firm handshake. "Let me know what you need around here," Rocky offered, "it can get rough sometimes."

"Thanks, I'll remember that," Winston returned with a smile, then released the grip and turned to Thunder. He grabbed the reins and mounted the stallion.

Rocky was assessing the gear on Thunder and commented, "I see those initials on your saddlebags read, WWC. What's the middle W stand for?"

Winston backed Thunder a bit, stopped him then smiled and said back, "Can you guess?"

"No!" the big man smiled.

"My momma's maiden name."

"Well, I'll be a…."

"No you won't, but I'll always be cursed with what I have to live up

17

to." Then he pulled back on the reins and gave a light spur to Thunder's flanks causing the horse to levade up on two legs. When the horse came down, Winston said, "Adios, my friend." Then he legged the stallion into a canter away from the house towards town.

'Imagine that," Rocky laughed out loud, "havin' those two names."

As he turned to go inside he bumped full face and body into Marilyn, who was now standing toe to toe with him. She asked, "What two names?"

"Why, Miss Marilyn, that man's name is Winston Winchester Colt."

CHAPTER THREE
A PERFECT FIT

Paddy McIrish looked out his shop window and saw the big white stallion tethered to the hitching rail. The snorting that had caught his attention sounded like a storm's announcement resonating against the glass panes. He saw no rider.

Coming from the boarded walk outside the shop Paddy felt vibrations from the heavy steps of someone about to enter the shop. He had built the place to do that. Even a moccasin clad intruder could not escape his creaking alarm system. His eyes watched the swinging bar-style doors and his hand lightly touched the butt of a Sheriff Model short barrel colt in a Denver Colorado made Heiser shoulder holster under his arm. Then he saw one boot under the doors. Then he saw the brim of the sweat stained plantation hat. Then he saw two piercing eyes peer over the top of one door. And then one hand went on top of the door. If two hands had been on top of the door, Paddy would have lowered his hand from his Colt.

Winston Colt pushed open the door with his right hand and entered sideways with a box under his left arm. Seeing one gun hand elevated and the other busy, Paddy lowered his gun hand, raised his head and said, "Looks like I was expecting you."

"You Mr. McIrish?" Winston asked with a smile.

"Aye, laddy," was the reply.

Winston set the package on the counter in front of the muscled, broad, redheaded gun shop owner. Paddy's cherubic face smiled.

"Ya 'ave the look a yer gran-father," Paddy commented.

"You knew him then," Winston beamed.

"Aye. I was a wee lad from the ol' country. His genius infected my soul. Boot that's anoother starry," he smiled, imparting a distant invitation to tell all at another time.

The box on the counter was wrapped in heavy waxed paper and had thick twine tied four squared tightly around it. Both men had their eyes on it as though it was a gift for each of them. The moment lingered and the anticipation of the inevitable opening caused them both to simply freeze. Each needed the other to encourage the unveiling.

The bar doors crashed open. Both men drew their guns. Big Thunder just snorted all over them and stood there. Paddy and Winston burst out in laughter.

"He's thirsty," Winston remembered. He led the stallion out the doors and tied him to the opposite rail where the water trough was.

When Winston reentered the shop, Paddy asked, "Af yer harse was so smart, whyn't he jus' go to the trough hisself?"

"Ah," Winston answered, "he doesn't think he's a horse. He had to make his point first."

Paddy laughed, soon joined by Misters Colt and Winchester's grandson who enjoyed the humor of his own comment. Then their eyes returned to the package on the counter.

"Ah bin ardered ta open tha package an inspect the goons," Paddy whispered.

"The guns are to be delivered to you, Mr. McIrish," Winston said, sliding a piece of paper towards the Irishman. "You sign this receipt and you do what you want."

McIrish took his quill from the ink stand, dipped it into the ink well and scribbled his signature across the dotted line. He quickly returned the feather to its place and deftly lifted a razor from his pocket, flipped it open and slit the string around the package. Just as deftly, he folded the razor and slipped it home. The string limped free, leaving the paper free to unfold.

Paddy took a deep breath. He carefully lifted the box and spread the paper off the box. He set the box down and carefully placed the brown wax wrapper aside, being careful not to make any additional creases in it.

"A collector I see," Winston commented with a smile.

"Aye, laddy, I like evra-thin original."

Winston was beginning to really like this man. He had class.

When the paper was removed it revealed another layer of thin, soft wood surrounding the box. Paddy raised a confused eyebrow.

"We do that now to protect the presentation box. We try to keep everything perfect when you get it," Winston informed. "I think it's called balsa wood. From South America, I believe."

McIrish did not reply. He was filled with anticipation. He pushed the spectacles back on the bridge of his nose, pulled the kerchief from his back pocket, wiped the sweat from his brow, returned the kerchief, then began to peel the balsa away from the box until it was free from all packaging. McIrish gulped.

Although he had ordered it, he had never seen Zebra-wood. It was magnificent with its rich, dark and light swirling stripes. And just as ordered, there was no plaque on the top. The box was so finely cut that he could not even see a line between the top and the bottom.

"I wooda paid ya the same fer tha box," he said, "it's pear-fect."

Winston smiled.

His hands shaking in a way that it never would if he faced an outlaw on the draw, he slowly began sliding the slip lock bar through the four holes. Unique and unusual, there was a small brass chain that attached to the bar, or pin, and he set it parallel to the bottom of the box.

"We did that so it could not be lost," Winston announced.

"Aye, a know, laddy. Valya keepin' all the parts toghetha. Got ta maintain the valya," Paddy acknowledged, "got ta maintain the valya."

Then Paddy closed his eyes and lifted the top of the box. Winston was intently looking at the box also, and then he heard Paddy take a deep breath. Paddy opened his eyes and met Winston's. Like children at Christmas, they both smiled and then looked immediately into the open box. Neither man said a word for a full minute.

The gleaming pistols were reclining barrels to butts in perfectly fitted velvet lined beds that outlined exactly the shape of the guns' nickel frames and cylinders in stark contrast to the blued barrels. Within the case and between the pistols were the two extra blue cylinders. There were twelve cartridges aligned along the top of the case. Paddy squinted as he moved closer and saw that the tip of each bullet had a stamped hallmark.

"The casings are polished brass, but, but," stuttered the awestruck Irishman, "the tips appear to be pure silver."

"We aim to please," Winston smiled proudly, "and I was told that the center of each tip is 24 karat gold. Just a little bonus. Hope your client likes it."

Paddy's trembling fingers lightly skimmed the pistols, first touching the ancient mastodon ivory grips. Winston heard him suck air as he perused the perfectly carved eagles that rose from the handles. He hesitated, then placed his finger inside one of the trigger guards. He raised the pistol up from the case letting the pistol fall upside down from his finger. He confirmed that an identical eagle was on the other side.

Winston's lips uttered a low winded wolf whistle.

"Pretty, ain't they?" the gunsmith muttered.

"Might be one of the best factory engraving jobs I've ever seen," Winston confirmed. "Don't recollect ever having seen an order for nickel frames with contrasting blued barrels, but that's why it's called Colt's Custom Gun Shop."

"Aye, and the coostomer wanted the extra blued cylinders so's he could practice his shootin' withoot puttin' a line on the nickel ones."

"Good idea," Winston nodded. "Most of these guns seldom, if ever get fired. They just sit and look pretty for collectors."

"Nay, not'n this neck 'o the woods. We don't 'ave nuthin' we doon't use…includin' ar' women!" he laughed.

Winston smiled broadly not just from the joke itself, but from the Irish brogue that so uniquely delivered it. He thought that he'd stay an extra day or two to get to know this interesting man. Maybe he'd even hear some new stories about his grandfather.

"Why are the trigger guards enlarged, do ya think?" Winston innocently asked.

Paddy McIrish looked up directly into Winston's eyes. He took off his glasses and said slowly, "The man don't 'av hands, he 'as da paws o' a grizzlay. Same reason why the grips are oversoized, too."

The story was getting interesting to Winston. He decided to definitely stay over and see how these characters blended together.

Paddy deftly removed the base pin from the first gun, removing the nickel cylinder. He then picked up a blued cylinder and dropped it into the frame and replaced the pin. He did the same with the other pistol. He layed them both back in their velvet beds. He untied his black apron and looped it over his head revealing a perfectly starched and ironed white dress shirt, neatly outlining a slight paunch, tucked into black wool slacks supported by bright red braces. He hooked the apron, then looked up at the cadre of holsters hanging from hooks on the wall. He grabbed a well worn twin fancy Buscadero holster rig that was a perfect fit for the 7-1/2 inch barrels. Then he deftly strapped it on and tied down the holsters to each thigh. He carefully picked up the first pistol and slid into each hole of its cylinder a .44 caliber cartridge which he had personally loaded. He did the same with the other pistol. That done, he placed the guns one in each holster and winked at Winston.

Paddy leaned forward and started spinning what Winston thought must be a wheel gear under the counter. Slowly, the cabinet and wall behind him parted, retreating into the wall to create an eight foot floor to ceiling gap in the cabinet, and a little better than a fifty foot long shooting range; targets and all. Winston beamed a big smile of approval. The target at the end of the shooting range was a six foot tall paper image of a gunman.

From a nearby hook, the gunsmith grabbed a hat and covered his balding head with what was a flat crown straight brim in black with a sterling silver band studded with turquoise. He then walked to the entry of the open cabinet door. Winston was impressed so far.

There were two raised balls of wood on the opposite counters going into the shooting range. Paddy placed his hands on each ball so that his arms spread like wings from his side. Neat trick, Winston thought, anticipating what was going to occur next.

When McIrish lifted his hands from the wooden balls, the paper gunfighter instantly moved forward as though on a spring; which it was. McIrish drew both guns quickly and emptied all twelve bullets into the target before it was three quarters of the way in front of him. The target then stopped right in front of him.

"Whoa," Winston gulped, "that was fantastic."

"Not r'lly," Paddy apologized, "I usually get 'im with all the bullets afore he's two thards the way."

"Hey, but I see twelve holes in that varmit, so you can't complain. Do you mind if I try?"

Paddy was already ejecting the spent shells from the cylinders and he said, "Sure."

When he had dumped all of the casings in a box he pulled out some gummed paper and put it over each of the holes in the target. Then he grabbed a handle that held the wire that ran from where the target was standing all the way to the back of the range and back to be attached to the top of the target. He pulled the handle which dragged the target to compress the light metal spring back to its catch point at the rear of the range. Then he invited, "Ye can come back 'o tha countar 'ere now, yoong man."

Winston walked in back of the counter and stood in front of the open range. He drew his left .45, half cocked the hammer and spun the cylinder to check that all the bullets were there then spun the weapon back in the holster. He did the same with the right. He placed his hands on the wooden balls and looked over to Paddy, who winked confirmation. Winston took a breath.

When Winston lifted his hand from the balls the target began its assault forward. Paddy saw only Winston's right hand move at first. Then he heard the first shot followed by what sounded like one continuous sound. The right gun spun back in its holster and the left one was drawn so quickly that Paddy wasn't sure what was happening. Then he heard one distinct shot and again, followed by one loud continuous noise. The target was only half way to Winston when he holstered the left Colt.

The gunsmith was perplexed. He walked over to the silhouette target of a man and saw 11 holes; all dead center; in the eyes.

"Whew," Paddy gasped, "never seed the like 'a that. But, there be only eleven hits. Me thinks ya may'a missed one."

"I doubt it," Winston replied confidently, as he lifted the right Colt from its holster then opened the loading gate and began ejecting shells.

"Ah, here it is," he smiled, handing a non-spent .45 caliber bullet to the gunsmith.

"Hmm, hang fire. Factory ammo, too," he mused. "Kinda validates yer fannin' method."

"Only used it once in real time," Winston said.

"Twelve?"

"Nah, only seven."

Paddy McIrish's face broke out in a very wide, Cheshire Cat grin. He just shook his head as he closed the cabinet doors to again hide his shooting range.

"I'd be obliged to buy a box of bullets from you, sir," Winston said, as the last spent cartridge ejected from his left Colt.

McIrish placed a worn looking box of live shells on the counter and said, "I know ya prabablee only use fact'ry ammo, boot, I loaded these here meeself. Nevar 'ad a missfoir. By the way, laddy, intrestin' rig there with woot seems ta be firm forms around the cylindars."

"Had 'em specialy made with steel to reinforce so the guns slip in and out the same every time." Then Winston smiled and reloaded his guns with the offered bullets, knowing that his life may depend on the gunsmith's telling the truth. He walked to the customer side of the counter once again to see that Paddy was wiping the powder away from the cylinders of the custom guns.

"Ah alrady sees a faint line on the cylinder fram the turnin'," he commented. "Boot, that ware ta be expected." He placed the pistols back in the case.

Winston felt the floor boards vibrate. He saw that Paddy was already looking at the doors and had his hand on the Colt under his armpit. Winton turned his head to the door and saw a huge head topped with a tall crowned white flat brimmed hat. The hat band was sterling silver and there was a big raw silver nugget in the center. The man's eyes were wide open and light blue and they peered over the swinging doors at the gunsmith and his customer.

Paddy invited, "Well, poosh them dars open, Buck, I gat year goons roit here."

Buck put his hands on the tops of the doors. Winston did a double take. He now saw why the trigger guards on the pistols he had brought were double the normal size; Buck's fingers were thick and long and hairy as a grizzly. The man almost filled the doorway as he pushed his body through to reveal a well tailored 3 piece grey pinstriped suit surrounding a perfectly starched white shirt where from its collar hung a leather string tie, or bolo, with a large sterling silver concha joining the strands together. In the middle of the concha was a fancy and deeply engraved letter "K."

Buck had a big smile on his face and proclaimed, "Happy birthday to me, and it is today. Whaddya think about them apples?" He was rubbing his paws together in joyful anticipation like a child at a party.

"This is Mr. Colt, Buck," McIrish introduced, "he personally brought yer goons fer ya from the fac'try. Winston, this is Mr. Krupp. Buck Krupp."

Winston lost sight of his hand when they shook and said, "Pleasure, sir. I know a Krupp family. They're German."

"That's true sir, and the pleasure is all mine," Buck gleamed back with a toothy smile surrounded by his perfectly trimmed beard and handlebar mustache. "My family is indeed in the arms business. I'm in the cattle business." Then he quickly turned his attention to the cased set of Colt pistols resting on the counter.

Winston watched as Buck spread his coat at the waist and placed his hands on his hips revealing on his right hip a cross draw holster containing a pearl handled nickel plated S&W Model 3 break top. Winston guessed right that it was a Russian .44.

Buck leaned over to capture in his view for the first time what he had ordered. There was dead silence in the store for a full minute until Winston and Paddy started to hear Buck's heavy breathing. Buck then pulled a white kerchief from his front pocket and wiped his eyes.

"These are Jim Dandy, simply Jim Dandy," he said. "Finally, something that a monster can hold with grace."

Buck then picked up both Colts from the case. They felt good to him; light in weight and balanced perfectly. He liked the standard 7-1/2 inch barrel length, too, because they were accurate both with targets and danger. He moved his trigger fingers around inside the guards and smiled. Then he let out what seemed to be a sigh of relief, "Ahhhhh, finally." Paddy and Winston looked at each other and smiled. Their client was happy.

Buck didn't do any fancy twirling, because he never practiced that. But, seeing that there was a faint line on the blued cylinders already, he cocked the hammers. "Whoops," he then said, realizing he had just broken a cardinal rule. He promptly checked both cylinders and found them to be empty at which point he again breathed a sigh of relief that he wasn't playing with loaded guns. He quickly put both pistols back to bed in their case.

"Time to celebrate, gentlemen," Buck announced. "If you'll join me at the hotel dining room, I'd be honored to buy you both dinner and the best champagne."

Paddy looked to Winston who nodded and smiled.

"I've gotta check in there anyway. I came in to Denver on the train and my gear was transferred to a stage, so it should have arrived already. Mind if I get cleaned up first?" Winston asked. "I had a run in with some pintos and a wild mustang mare with a red mane a while ago."

"Ah, ye met mistress Maarelyn, then," Paddy figured.

"I did."

"What was the occasion?" Buck wondered, squinting his eyes to listen carefully.

"I'll tell you over dinner," Winston answered as he waved goodbye and exited the doors towards his horse.

The two men remaining each stopped a swinging door and peered over the top of them to see Winston already mounted and headed for the nearby stable.

CHAPTER FOUR

THE GATHERING

Winston bounded down the stairs to the hotel lobby. His curly hair was freshly combed and still wet. He wasn't wearing his hat and he had changed his riding clothes to all black with the overcoat tapered to accentuate his narrow waist and broad shoulders. His twin rig holster cradling the Colts was thrown over his shoulder.

The desk clerk nodded acknowledgment and said, "Evening, Mr. Colt. Your party is awaiting you in the dining room."

He nodded back and stopped to look around. The hotel was nicely appointed. It could have been in the best area of Denver, Winston thought. The lobby had a high ceiling with what looked like a real European crystal chandelier looming in the center. The décor was red and black. The place looked elegant, but very masculine like a men's club, or even a high end brothel. In any case, it appeared that no expense had been spared.

Winston sauntered to the entry of the dining room and looked for his dinner partners. He saw them dead center of the room at a circular table. Buck, Paddy and what looked like a badged lawman were talking. Buck saw him and waved.

Winston arrived at the table and immediately approached the one person he did not know, extended his right hand and announced, "I'm Winston Colt, sir."

The man had long grey streaked hair, a craggy experienced face and one shoulder harnessed pistol under each armpit. Winston noticed that one seemed to be a Colt Sheriff's model with a two inch barrel, and the other a break-top Smith & Wesson. The man arose, and shook Winston's hand, responding, "Micah Curtis. Territorial marshal. It's a pleasure, son."

Winston thought he could tell a lot about a man from his grip. The marshal's was firm but not overdone. His hand had hit Winston's in a perfect fit as though it could just as easily have grabbed either one of his holstered pistols with the same exact precision. Winston smiled, they let go, and Winston went to the only vacant chair at the table.

"Nice to meet you, too, marshal."

"I'll need a statement from you, son. And sooner than later, if you don't mind," Micah added. "I hear it was quite a scene out there."

"Absolutely, sir," Winston affirmed, "and indeed it was," he ended as he took his gun belt, rolled it and placed it between his boots under his chair and sat down and then proclaimed, "I'm hungry, gentlemen. What's the house special?"

The three other men smiled.

"Oh, I see," Winston remembered, "we're in cattle country. Guess its steak."

"Actually, I ordered up a whole prime rib for the table," Buck announced. "It's from my spread of angus. Tender and red, it is."

"Ol' Book 'ere be a moight modest, as ye can tell. 'e owns the cattle and the 'otel," Paddy interjected. "If we sit 'round long enough, 'e'll be tellin' us 'is loif starry, too."

"And an interesting one it is, actually," the marshal chimed in.

The tuxedoed waiter arrived at the table and removed the empty champagne bottle from the ice bucket, replacing it with a fresh one. Another waiter placed a fresh flute in front of Winston, took the full bottle from the bucket and held the bottle over Winston's glass.

"Yes, thank you," Winston said, to which his glass was appropriately filled. He raised his glass to the others and took a sip.

"I propose a toast," Buck announced, raising his glass, quickly followed by the others. "Here's to true intentions, justice, and straight shooting."

"Especially with a Colt firearm," Winston joked.

"Hear, hear!" the others agreed in unison to the clink of glasses.

As they sipped, the wait staff rolled out to them a large serving table with a large half globed sterling silver cover atop it. When the globe was lifted, the smell of beef, potatoes, carrots, onions and juice filled their nostrils and made their mouths drip with hunger. The prime rib roast was magnificent. The waiter nodded at Winston.

"The center rarest for me, please," came Winston's request to which a bone in slice of no less than two pounds of meat was placed under his nose. His eyes closed to savor the smell.

"Aye, seer, oil taike the end o' that dear departed lad weir the garlic be so thick it'd farce tha devil 'imsel' aback ta 'is lair," Paddy said with childlike glee.

"Medium for me," said the Marshal.

Then the waiter chimed in to ask Buck, "I expect you'll have the usual cut, sir?" and Buck nodded with a smile.

The vegetables were placed around the table for each to take at his leisure and dishes of multiple calibers of to-taste horseradish was set to dare the bravest to water their eyes and snort like bulls from the burn.

Among men there is no need for courtesy and cordiality in the face of such bounty. They all dug in without a word.

Winston was about halfway through his side of beef when his eye caught the sight of white and red entering the room. Lifting his head he saw a dazzling sight. It was a lady-ed up Marilyn Montgomery flowing into the room. Her red hair was gleaming and clean and the only other color to her was in her stream deep blue eyes that flashed from milky white skin which matched the purity of the long white dress she was wearing. She was striking, he thought.

The other men did not at first see her, but they caught Winston's body language changing and turned towards the entrance of the dining room. Each man grabbed his cloth napkin and wiped his lips clean and then sipped from a glass of water. The lady was headed for their table. The men rose. A dazed and surprised Winston quickly brushed his lips with his napkin and quickly elevated up with them.

"Why gentlemen," Marilyn greeted, "y'all needn't have gone to all that trouble for little ol' me."

The men smiled and nodded anyway.

"Hello, there...Mr. Winchester-Colt," she said to Winston respectfully, to which he could only nod and blush as the other men looked at him curiously.

"You've met Mr. Colt?" Buck asked.

"Yes, I have, Buck. Yes, indeed I have," she confirmed leaving an air of mystery in her answer. Buck was obviously bothered.

"Would you care to join us, Marilyn," Buck offered.

"That would be simply charming, thank you. But, please, there are two of us; me and my escort. Is that acceptable to you?"

"Jonathan," Buck waved and ordered to the head waiter, "Please set two more places for Miss Montgomery and Mr. Mountain."

The room buzzed with service immediately. Marilyn was seated between Buck and the marshal and the other seat and setting was placed between Paddy and Winston.

"Well, what is the occasion?" Marilyn asked, taking a sip from her champagne glass and looked around to gaze for an instant directly into the eyes of each man.

Winston now noticed here trademark hair still covered the right side of her face and partially even the right eye so it appeared to be peering through gauze. When her head moved, the hair near her face did not. He thought that was strange and wondered how she did it.

To the lady's question Buck reached under his chair and placed the gun box on his lap and opened it. Marilyn smiled and her eyes opened wide.

"So that's what Mr. Colt brought to town," she said.

"Pretty, aren't they?" Buck beamed, "And finally something to fit my paws."

Everyone at the table smiled at that reply.

"Mr. Mountain," the marshal announced as the escort arrived to the table, "I hope you brought your appetite with you 'cause this is the best prime rib I think I ever 'et."

"Hey, Micah. Yes, I did bring it with me. Good to see you. And, Mr. Krupp," he nodded acknowledgement, "Winston."

"So, Rocky, how do you know Mr. Colt?" Buck asked.

"Had a shoot out a few years back. Friendly one, of course," he said, turning to the waiter, "I'll have the rare center cut, thanks."

"We were on the same side of the law, Mr. Krupp," Winston jokingly reassured.

"I'd like to hear about dat vun," Buck slipped into a slight German accent.

Winston had no idea the man was not born in the United States until that language faux pax. The others were not alarmed but Marilyn's left eyebrow raised. Winston was sure he wanted to stay awhile now that there seemed to be some intrigue in town.

"Anyway, Buck," Marilyn said, "I like your new guns. They're very pretty."

"I do agree," Buck replied, recovering his composure and placing the box again under his chair.

As Marilyn and Rocky were eating, Micah couldn't wait any longer to clear up the mysteries of the table.

"Okay," he asked, "I'm the law around hear and I wanna hear how you all are connected. I need evidence."

"Well, to tell the truth," Winston offered, "I shot Miss Montgomery's horse, she paid me six hundred dollars, I met my old shooting match acquaintance, Rocky, at the Double M, and then I delivered the guns to Mr. Krupp, here. That about covers it."

There was silence at the table. Marilyn and Rocky were smiling, trying not to show that their mouths were full of meat.

"So, young man," Paddy queried, "ya shot a harse?"

"I did, sir. Ya had ta be there. A thousand pounds of paint at full gallop comin' straight at ya, and only ten yards from where you're a standin'. The rider is firing forty five slugs that are hittin' yer holster. What's a city slicker ta do?"

"I guess you could have ducked," Rocky said, deadpan.

Everyone at the table laughed out loud for a full minute, spitting food and snorting champagne. Each had a picture of the event in their mind and each probably would have done the same thing.

"I hope it was that bastard stallion he shot," Buck directed to Marilyn.

"You hated him, didn't you?" she answered. "In fact it was ol' Danger."

"Danger he was. Especially when he bit that chunk out of the back of my arm," Buck added.

"He was jealous and didn't want you near me," Marilyn taunted.

Buck raised his eyebrows, but did not pursue the challenge. A conversation about jealousy and envy was not what he wanted to discuss in the company at this table. He placed the last bite of meat on his fork, dipped it into the hottest raw horse radish, then it disappeared into his mouth. His eyes watered and his nostrils leaked water but he did not show pain.

"You can tell a lot about a man by the cut of meat a man picks," Winston said to break the silence. "My grandpappy used to say that rare means a man is bold and fearless and will take chances with women, medium means a man likes his women seasoned, and well done indicates a man has tried both and eats alone."

"Alone, Mr. Colt? That makes no sense at all," Marilyn queried coyly.

"Well, ma'm, I think he knew that."

The men at the table went into hysterics. The other patrons in the restaurant caught the fever of laughter and didn't even know why.

When the room recovered to basic restaurant chatter, Marilyn directed to Micah, "Oh, I did mean to tell you that we brought three bodies in to the undertaker. Mr. Colt shot them all."

To Micah's raised eyebrows, Winston beamed a big, Cheshire cat smile.

"Only three?" Micah quipped. "I knew that…obviously."

"May, I explain," Winston interceded.

"No need, son. Fill me in tomorrow. If you had to shoot a horse, even a mean one, you probably had good reason to shoot the men."

Winston shrugged.

"So, Mr. Krupp," Paddy said, "Da ya still 'ave them big cigoars?"

Buck waved to the maitre'd, and made a gesture with his hand to his mouth.

"Did anyone ever notice that Paddy seems to mix his Irish and Scottish accents?" Rocky offered out of the blue.

"O, an' ye know the deference?" Paddy defended.

"Indeed I do, sir. I served with the 79th New York Volunteer Infantry during the great war between the states."

"Wall, aye knew ye' were a great shot with a roifle, but that I deedn't know that bit o' news, sir."

"You've worked on my Henry, right?" Rocky continued, "Well, the 79th started using the .69 caliber smoothbore musket, but I had heard about the Enfield .577 rifle and got them to switch."

"And how did you do that?" Buck asked.

"Well, to be honest, I was one of the men who cleaned the guns. I mentioned it to one of the lieutenants and he challenged my expertise. Well, no one else but me hit the bull's-eye from two hundred yards with the musket, so I gained my credibility then. When we lost too many men at Bull Run, they believed me. I stood toe to toe with the infantry and shot and loaded along side those men. They kind of adopted me as a Scot after that."

"The Germans had more troops than any other foreign country, so I know a little about that history," Buck interjected. "If what you say is true, where's your kilt?"

"Ah, the tartan kilt is tucked away. You should have seen when we wore them during battles with *me* running right along side of them. It gave new meaning to the words '*black-Irish*.' That's how I know that Paddy is Ulster-Irish. He's a protestant of Irish and Scottish descent."

"Here an' I thought ya were only the best shot in *this* territory," Paddy said.

Rocky smiled.

"I've seen him shoot," Winston confirmed, "and out of range of my pistols I would not want to be against him."

"Apparently you aren't too bad yourself with a Winchester, Mr. Colt," Marilyn chimed in.

"I'll still defer to mister..." he hesitated, "Mountain is it? Rocky... Mountain?"

"Well, it's only one mountain. I don't claim to be lofty enough for it to be the entire range," Rocky answered, adding, "and who else do we know who is named for a rifle *and* a pistol? Now *that* is lofty."

"Can we change the subject?" Winston asked.

"Why, Mr. Colt? Is there something else we should know?" Buck quizzed seriously.

"Self explanatory, sir. It's all self explanatory," Winston answered.

"So," Marilyn broke in wanting to further enliven the conversation, "Who is the best shot at the table?"

No one dared answer, because no one really knew. However, each had his own opinion.

"Since you all seem to be deaf, dumb and mute at this point, I think we need to have a contest," she challenged.

"Well, ain't it jus' loik a filly to challenge a herd a stallions," Paddy replied, "but, ya know, we've not 'ad such a thing 'appen in at least five elk moltins."

"I can see what these pistols you made for me can do, then," Buck gleefully rejoiced.

"That's a great idea and we'll have it in town, here," Micah added, "and I'll regulate the event. How about in two weeks, so's we can let everyone in the territory know."

"You have a telegraph yet in this place?" Winston asked.

"Yes, Mr. Colt, it's located in the third cave outside of town," Buck joked.

"Beg your pardon, sir," Winston said, "I should have guessed by the quality of your hotel. I'll wire the folks and see if they'll contribute something unique. It would be a good promotion for our business."

A bottle of cognac arrived at the table accompanied by a humidor of cigars. Each person, including the lady, picked their favorite dimension and lit up.

"My fadder youst ta say," Buck began after blowing a long puff of smoke into the room, "and I vill try to translate frum da German as best I can, that 'ven da cigar ees lit an' da cognac is pourt, da night ees very short.'"

"What does that mean?" Micah asked.

"Damned if I know," he laughed.

CHAPTER FIVE

Storm Clouds Gather

Winston exited the hotel and headed towards the stable. He had missed Big Thunder. It was nearly ten in the morning and he had understandably overslept. It had been a long night after all. The horse would be mad at him, he thought.

"Carrots", he reminded himself and headed for the grocery.

A boy about twelve years old, medium height, shaggy black hair, long fingers and neatly dressed as a storekeeper and with a checkered apron was pounding a nail into a post when Winston exited the store with Thunder's treat.

"What's on the poster, son," Winston asked. The boy moved out of the way so Winston could read aloud, "Shooting Contest. Pistols or Rifles, Speed – Accuracy – Horseback. Saturday – November 17 – 9am. Entry Fee: $20 per Event."

"Yes, sir," the young man said, "And I'm gonna enter, too."

"I like confidence, young man," Winston complimented, "what's your name."

"Jedidiah Johnson, sir. And I'm a pistol shooter."

"That means you're going to shoot against me," Winston said with a wink and a smile.

"That's fine sir, I can hold my own. I'm what my Pa calls, a natural."

"I like that. A natural. Maybe we can talk about that before the contest."

"Oh, I don't know sir, I wouldn't want to give away any secrets."

"Son, my name is Winston Winchester Colt. I represent the Colt Firearms company. I would be proud to give you some tips and maybe you could even beat me."

"Wow, well, maybe we could," the boy reconsidered while checking out the rig the stranger was wearing as his eyes widened like twenty dollar gold pieces.

"Okay, Jed…is it okay to call you that," Winston asked respectfully to a quick nod from the boy, "then I'll look you up in a day or so. Right now I have to take care of my best friend."

"Does he live here? Maybe I know him."

"Well, he does get around and has quite the personality, but I doubt you know him."

"What's his name?"

"Big Thunder."

Jedidiah looked puzzled for a moment and then smiled widely.

"It's your horse, isn't it?"

"Yes, sir. Best darn stallion I have ever had the privilege of teaming up with. He's a Spanish Andalusian, all the way from Spain. And what a personality he has, too. I'll introduce you to him sometime. He's pretty smart."

"That would be Jim Dandy, sir. I'll look forward to that as well."

"See ya," Winston finished, then shook the boy's hand and headed for the livery.

BIG THUNDER SPOKE LOUDLY WHEN he saw Winston enter the barn. Knowing of his friend's impatience, a carrot was immediately produced to bribe the stallion. Thunder bit it in half and happily chomped his prize. Thunder also nodded his head to show he was still peed off.

"Aw, ya still love me," Winston growled as he scratched behind the big horse's ears.

"Glad you finally got here. I thought he was gonna jump the stall," complained Horace Magee, the thickly muscled blacksmith.

Winston opened the stall door and saw that Thunder had scraped a good size hole in front of the inside door of his stall.

"I think he was diggin' my grave there," Winston said. "He does that when he's mad at me."

"Not to worry," the blacksmith understood, "he's been a pretty good boy. He's pretty nice for a stud. Seems to like kids, too."

"Yeah, I know."

"My son cleans the stalls. No trouble at all, and…"

"Hi, pa," the tall red haired lad chimed in as he entered from the back of the livery.

"This is Dude. He's my boy," Horace introduced.

"Well, you don't look like no dude ta me, son," Winston offered along with his outstretched hand.

"It's 'cause I like to wear a bowler hat they call me that, sir," the boy answered, taking the man's hand with a manly squeeze. "Very pleased to meet you sir. I sure do admire your horse. He's a real pip."

"Pip?" Winston asked.

"Some new jargon. These kids are changin' their lingo every week," the blacksmith apologized.

"Okay. I guess I was young once," Winston replied with a smile.

"I hear we're havin' a shooting contest in a couple of weeks," Horace said.

"Word sure gets out fast around here," Winston answered. "Quicker than a rooster in hen house…so to speak."

"I know who you are Mr. Colt. Me an' Jedidiah are gonna sign up. He's a lefty and I shoot with my right hand. We been practicin' a lot, and…"

"Now don't go braggin' on yerself now, son," Horace interrupted.

"Sorry, pa, but I'm just excited to show everyone what I can do," the boy said excitedly. "I bin' reloadin' my own ammo, just like Mr. Mc Irish showed me.

"I like that in a man," Winston cut in, "confidence. A willingness to prove a man's worth rather than just a brag gives the man value. I can't wait to see you boys in action."

"Can you really fan five shots with one swipe?" Dude asked.

"Geez, guess Mr. McIrish is the local telegraph here, too. Paddy obviously blabbed what he saw."

"Will you show me, sir?"

"Now, hold on there, son. Mr. Colt is here to get his horse and not to be your teacher," Horace scolded.

"I told your pard over there, Jedidiah is it, that I'd show him a trick or two, so I guess when the time comes you can join in."

"That's very accommodatin' of ya sir," Horace thanked.

"No problem, now let's see what this old white monster feels like doin' today."

Winston took a prancing and snorting Thunder by the halter and led him out of the stall.

"He's a right proud lookin' stallion, Mr. Colt," Horace commented. "Dynamic. Yessir. Dynamic."

"Thanks Horace. A horse like him kinda humbles any mortal man."

"I like him, too," Dude piped in. "He's kind, but scary."

"Yup," Winston agreed.

Winston led him to the tie up post and hooked the lead line into the iron eyelet. He went to grab a brush and hoof pick.

"I'll do that for you, Mr. Colt," the boy offered.

"Thanks, son, but I like this part," Winston informed with a wink. "It's where you and the horse start your relationship for the day. He knows you're personally going to care for his wellbeing."

Horace waved for Dude to come with him out of the barn. He knew when a man and his friend needed some time together. As many horses as Horace had touched in his life, he'd seen just as many people who had either bonded with their horses as a friend of importance, or else treated them as just another tool to get through life. Horace liked this young man, if for nothing else than the bond he had with this big Andalusian stallion.

When Thunder was hoof picked, brushed, talked to, saddled, bridled, talked to, then mounted, they rode out the front of the livery barn.

Horace and Dude were watching from the back of the barn as the horse and rider exited the front.

"He didn't lunge that stallion or nuthin'," Dude whispered to his father.

"Spirit, my boy," Horace replied, "Some of us like to feel that real masculine spirit between our legs a'fore it's ridden out o' the horse on the trail. And it's a good thing to do when yer young, my boy, 'cause someday some human filly may never let you experience that agin'."

"Whaddya mean, pa?"

"Just a sorta joke, my boy. You've plenty o' time to learn them things."

WINSTON DECIDED TO RIDE OUT to pay his respects at the Double M ranch, but he only made it half way before he saw a cloud of dust in the distance coming right towards him. Being now cautious in this territory he pulled his carbine from the scabbard and levered in a round; then he returned it to the scabbard. He drew both pistols and again checked that they were fully loaded. Then he felt around his holster belt to be sure all the loops were full of slugs. He already knew he was fully loaded up, but now he was confident. He stopped and waited for the rider to grow nearer.

It was Rocky. He could see the big man was not riding straight in the saddle. He let Thunder move forward at a jog to meet the rider. Rocky's horse did not slow from his gallop speed. Winston stopped Thunder when Rocky neared, but Rocky went right by them. Rocky had no hat and he was bleeding.

Just then a loud cracking sound surrounded them and a dark grey cloud blocked out the sun. The lightning bolt landed a hundred yards away causing Thunder's mane to stand up like a waxed hairdo. True to his name, however, he shrugged it off as the cracking and rumbling then vibrated the earth. The ensuing silver dollar sized drops of rain flattened the mane, and everything else not rigid. Winston turned him in the direction of the stampeding horse with Rocky on its back.

The rain was dense. Winston squinted to get a view of the rider when he saw the rear of Rocky's horse hit the road. It seemed that Rocky had gained control because he waited until the horse picked up its rear to sit up straight again. And then Rocky fell off the horse.

Thunder was coaxed to a slow trot until they came upon the scene of Rocky in the mud. His horse was nearby, dazed and confused.

Winston dismounted. He cradled Rocky's head in his arm and placed his own hat above the man's face so as to shield him from the rain.

"Miss Montgomery," Rocky spat, "she's, she's been…"

"What's that man? What are you trying to say?" Winston worriedly inquired.

"We were finishing breakfast when they burst in wanting the money," he gasped. "By god, though, I didn't let 'em have it. They tried to beat it outta me, but I don't know the combination to the safe. Then they started on Miss M. But she showed 'em her face and that backed 'em away, it did. By god, they were scared." He started to cough.

Winston lifted him to clear the phlegm in his throat and asked, "Where is she?"

"Don't know. They took her away. Just took her away."

Winston gathered the horses. He helped Rocky onto his own horse then mounted Thunder. They were all really wet. Cold wet. Winston worried for Rocky that the chilly rain would make him ill. They trotted the thirty minutes back to town directly to the doctor's office.

"He's tough. He'll be alright," the doctor reassured. "Better get yourself dry, though," he directed to Winston.

"Gotta talk to Micah." Then he walked out the door.

Walking across the street to the Marshal's office didn't dry him out as the rain continued to pound everything. Thunder was tied in front, but being a horse with centuries of developed rain deflecting hide he just stood relaxed resting on three legs. Winston didn't worry.

"Marshal," he announced opening the door to a pot belly stove radiating comfort, "we've got a problem."

Micah held up a letter.

"Ransom?" Winston figured.

"Yep."

MICAH CURTIS WAS A MARSHAL of distinction. He carried his Schofield and the Colt with confidence, and he could skin both fast enough. But more important, he was deliberate. He could let the bullets of his opponent wiz by while he took careful aim and hit his mark. He had tamed many a burgeoning town with his easy yet tough way. That was why he'd been hired by the township of Sagebrush Springs. They wanted order as they developed their area into a rich cattle, mining and farming community. The townspeople wanted it all, but without pain. By hiring Micah they figured the bad guys would just stay away. However, this was going to be their first experience with trouble, Micah thought. He was disappointed that he couldn't avoid this hiccup. But, he thought, he would cancel that out by saving Marilyn Montgomery.

"Before we discuss the rescue plan, I got a question for you," Winston said, taking off his dripping hat. "Rocky said that Marilyn showed them her face and they backed off. So?"

Micah hesitated. "Okay. From what I hear someone tried to take advantage of her when she was a youngster. The guy had a gun to her face and she grabbed it. Now, it's just rumor, but she grabbed the barrel of the gun and moved it away but the guy pulled the trigger and the bullet ripped her face. That's the story I heard."

"Woo. Tough girl," Winston said.

"That ain't all. She rolled the guy back and ripped his eyes out with her finger nails. He bled to death. That's the rumor anyway."

There was silence for a full minute.

"Posse?" Winston asked.

"You, me, and everyone else will come, too."

Micah took a long barrel Model 73 Winchester from the rack of guns and walked out the door. On the boarded walk outside his office were three other men about to enter his office. Micah and Winston nearly collided with them.

"Men," Micah became official, "you're all deputized. Get your horses and guns and meet us at the livery in five minutes. I gotta talk to Rocky Mountain, then we go."

All were covered by their waxed dusters. No one complained about the rain, the cold or the job.

CHAPTER SIX

TOGETHER WE RIDE

———————

The posse rode through the rain, thunder, and lightning to the Double M ranch house. There was one lantern lit with light coming from the barn.

Micah walked his horse over to see who was there. The others had their rifles unsheathed.

Still on his horse he grabbed the wooden handle and his gate trained steed side passed slowly as they pulled one of the tall doors open. A lighted lantern was sitting in the center of the barn between the two rows of horse stalls. Not seeing anything, he backed away his horse and drew his pistol. Then he nudged the horse forward and opened the other door.

"Come out now," he yelled over the pounding raindrops that were beating like a drum on the roof of the barn, "there's a dozen of us here and you're surrounded."

A young man of about sixteen years emerged cautiously. His hands were up about shoulder high. He resembled Rocky. In fact, Micah new him to be Rocky's son.

"Mr. Micah, sir, I'm scared," the young man proclaimed.

Micah replaced the pistol in its holster and assured, "Abraham, your dad's okay with the doc. You need to tell me what happened."

In the main house the marshal and his posse sat by a warm fire and sipped hot coffee. They listened to Abraham's account of the incident.

"Did you recognize any of the men," Micah asked.

"No, sir," Abraham recalled, "they all had on black masks and black hats is all I remember. One of them had a fancy holster rig with a different kind of gun."

"How so?" Winston butted in because that was his business.

"Well, it had carved stag horn grips and was blued on the frame but had a nickel silver cylinder."

Winston was silent; shocked at the similarity.

"The man drew the pistol and fired once, then he spun it back in the holster," Abraham added.

"Micah," Winston whispered, "that sounds like the gun I delivered to Paddy for Buck except for the grips."

"I know. Now what do I do?" Micah whispered back. "Just don't tell nobody yet."

Winston nodded.

"My daddy yelled at me to run when he saw the men coming," Abraham offered. "I wanted to stay, but he wouldn't let me."

"We know," Micah confirmed, "your dad told us."

"I want to go with you," Abraham insisted, "I need to avenge my father. I can shoot near as well as he can, sir. And Miss Montgomery, she's been, well, a friend to me. Doesn't treat me like some people do. I need to find her."

"The best thing you can do is take care of this place until your pa comes back. The Double M needs a man until things get back to normal. We'll find Miss M. Don't you worry about that."

"Yes, sir, I'll do that," the young man agreed.

Micah pulled Winston to the side and said, "I'm thinking we should wait 'til morning to head out."

"Why don't you all do that and I'll do some scouting for tracks and stuff," Winston offered. "Who is the best tracker you've got?"

"Actually, that would be Abraham and his dad. They know this area best, 'specially the mountains."

"Who's gonna stay here, then?"

"Marilyn has her hands and their families in houses in outlying areas. They'll show up for work tomorrow and one of 'em can stay here."

Winston pulled Abraham aside and said, "Get your rifle, son, you're going with me. Saddle up a horse and get your duster on. We're gonna ride in ten minutes."

THE HEAVY RAIN HAD LET UP, but a mist was so heavy that water was still rolling off Winston and Abraham's oiled dusters as the early morning light lit a dull glow behind the clouds. Abraham's horse was a big plow-horse, probably a Persheron, Winston thought. The boy could handle the horse fine and his tack and dress were appropriate for a hunter-tracker in the Rocky Mountains. Funny, Winston thought, but that was appropriate.

The muddy tracks of several horses leaving the MM ranch headed in a direction Winston really didn't really want to go. The misted mountain range in the near distance would not be friendly country for them and could only help the kidnappers. Thunder slipped slightly on the muddy path, proving his point, but the sure footed stallion quickly regained his prideful strut.

A few miles to the base of the mountain, nearing what looked like a canyon, they came across what appeared to be a temporary camp site. A fire was smoldering and double the amount of hoof tracks was evident. A red dress was thrown over a rock.

"Looks like they had her change clothes," Abe commented.

"And, whaddya think, they had pack horses waiting ?" Wintson added.

"Appears as so, by the deeper hoof prints. Looks like they may be headed up to the hunters cabins higher up."

"You know that country?"

"Yessir. My dad and I hunt there every year. Loads of elk. We bring the meat back and smoke it. Lots of cougars and wolves, too, though."

"How far is the first cabin?

" 'bout half day's ride, I guess. Then there are others at half day intervals. But it's easy to get lost if you don't know the canyons and trails."

"And you do, I reckon."

"Yup."

"I think we're going to need some help, otherwise we could end up in an ambush. Can you tell me how to get to the first cabin?"

"Maybe I should go up there and you go get the others," Abe suggested.

Winston looked at the young man dead in the eyes and knowing the answer asked anyway, "Ever kill a man, son?"

"Er...no, sir."

"Tell me how to get there."

"Sure, the first cabin is easy."

BACK IN TOWN, MICAH ASKED Paddy to come along. He wanted to question Buck. The two of them rode to Buck Krupp's ranch about ten miles outside of town.

It was still dark but a break in the clouds allowed the half moon to illuminate the stone mansion. As the men rode up the winding road to the home Paddy commented, "Loukes like a bluedy German church it does."

"Yeah, like one them eerie gothic ones in the picture books," Micah agreed.

A bolt of lightning hit somewhere in back of the house scaring the horses to stiffen, eyes wide and ears to the sky, when its scattering light caused shadows to appear to jump out at them. The thunder crackled then moved in a long echoing roar. The horses turned. Their experienced riders were able to turn them back, but both men were worried that the muddy ground could cause them all to be on their backs. Luckily that wasn't the case.

There was a carriage barn near the entrance and a couple of stalls for visitors' horses. Micah and Paddy tied theirs up and charged up the stone steps through the now pouring rain. Micah's neck craned all the way up the two story door to take in the intimidating height of it. He saw large stone gargoyles diverting rainwater away from the doorway. He looked back down and grabbed with both hands the heavy door knocker that was in the shape of a cannon barrel supported by two spoked wheels. He lifted the cannon barrel and let it fall three times. Each time the door knocker hit the door it sounded like the boom of a real cannon. Micah wondered which was louder; the noise from the knocker or the thunder. Slowly the door opened.

"Velcome," the skin bald monocled man offered, "please come in out of da veatha."

Micah shook the water of his coat and took off his hat. Paddy followed suit.

"Let me take 'dem, ya?" the doorman said.

"Thanks, Reinhard," Micah acknowledged, knowing the man as Krupp's personal assistant and a relative of some kind.

When both men had given up their wet coats and hats, they could see straight ahead to the main hall across the foyer. The large Gothic arched opening under the second level mezzanine was flanked by two wide semi-circular stairways with marble balustrades that curved from the bottom of the entry about fifty feet apart.

"I've been in this place only once before during daylight," Micah whispered to Paddy, "but only in the office over there to the right. That door ahead of us was closed."

"Aye, me, too," Paddy whispered back, craning his neck to look up to the top of the open portal, "it's a bit scary at night."

When Reinhardt had hung their coats and hats on the heads of protruding brass griffins, he led them towards the main hall beyond the entry. From where they stood about to enter the great-room, they could see that the fireplace was about fifteen feet in width. As they passed through the entrance the fireplace dominated their view, as was intended. Their eyes focused on the burning pine logs cut to fit the width of the fireplace, ablaze with narrower aspen logs used as kindling. The mantle was at the height of a tall man. It was a huge crackling hot fire. They seemed to be drawn to it and its warmth. Again, gargoyles and griffins greeted them, with varying fearsome expressions and holding up the mantle with clawed hands and muscled arms. Pipes connected from under the fire to the gargoyles mouths heated the air inside them that was blowing hot breath from their open mouths.

The Krupp coat of arms filled the space above the mantle. Both men just stood there in front of the fireplace, looking at the fire, the coat of arms, the gargoyles, the fire…

"Gentlemen," came a booming greeting from nearby, "Welcome to my humble cabin."

The men turned and saw Buck Krupp holding in one hand a cigar and a snifter with something reddish swirling slowly.

"Buck, ya got quite a place here," Micah complimented.

"Nothing like where I grew up. You should see what the family has in the Alps of Germany," Buck puffed.

"One can only imagine," Paddy mumbled, as he looked around and up at the awesome cathedral-like room with stained glass windows and tree sized beams.

"So, what brings you here?" Krupp asked. "Oh, how rude of me. May I offer you some warmed cognac and perhaps a smoke?" He stepped in front of the fireplace where there were andirons warming bottles.

"Nah, that's alright," Micah refused.

"Don' mind if ah doo," Paddy accepted, picking up a snifter and allowing Buck to pour him some fine imported cognac. He took the cigar offered, bit off the end and from the fire took a small twig of burning pine bough and lit it.

"Well, Buck," Micah, started, "seems Marilyn Montgomery's been kidnapped.

Buck's face seemed to turn white. Micah made note of it.

"Why?" Buck asked.

"Ransom."

"Vat do dey vant?" he nervously began losing his non-accented English.

"Money, of course, and lots of it."

"How can I help?" Buck asked. "I, I can't believe dis!

"Well, first can you get that set of guns you picked up from Paddy yesterday?" Micah asked.

"My guns? Vell, vell, I guess so. But, I don't understand vhy…vell, no, come to zink of it. Dare not hea." Buck admitted.

"Hmm."

"I zent dem to be engraved. Vhy do you vant to see dem guns, should I ask?"

"Well, seems Abraham saw one of the kidnappers with a Colt that matches the description of yours."

"Marshal, do you zink I would have anyting ta do mit zumting like dis?"

"Hope not, Buck, but I gotta ask. It's my job."

"I understand," Buck said, as he turned and went out the doors to the entry where he met and began chatting with Reinhardt.

"Whaddya think?" Paddy whispered to Micah. Micah placed a finger over his own lips.

Buck hurriedly stepped back into the main hall and confronted the two men.

"I've sent for the guns to be returned immediately," Buck said, having calmed down from the initial shock to regain his non-accented English.

"Good first step," Micah said, "but I gotta ask you straight out. Do you know anything about Marilyn's kidnapping?"

Buck took a deep breath then said calmly, "No, sir."

"It's a known fact that you want her ranch and she won't sell," Micah went on. "So, that could figure in, don't you think?"

"Sir, we Krupps don't need to steal anything, and I...."

"Whoa, hold on there Buck," Micah interrupted, "don't get excited. It's my job to ask and it's your obligation to answer. Don't take offense and I ain't accusin' you of stealing anything. I'm just investigating for some reason why anyone would want to do this thing."

"Okay, Micah," Buck began to calm down, "no I couldn't imagine why this would happen. In fact, I will confess, I asked Marilyn to marry me once."

"I never knew that," Micah replied surprised.

"No one does. She's very discreet. She knows how I feel and all the money, land minerals or anything could not make me want to harm her."

"Minerals? What minerals?"

"Coal and oil. You didn't know that?

"Nope. I know about the gold and silver is all. But, oil?"

Buck raised his eyebrows and informed, "Oil is the next gold, sir. The machine age is coming and oil will be the key to it."

"And Marilyn's property has it?" Micah reasoned.

"Yes."

"Well, there's a motive, I guess. But all the ransom asked for is money. Lot's of it."

"How much?"

"Two hundred fifty thousand in gold."

"Nobody has that much, unless...." Buck stopped, "she sold the mineral rights to get it."

"Well, Buck," Micah finished, "we got a posse up and we're going after them."

"Of course, but I vill go mit you..." Buck offered, "and..."

"No, I think I'd rather you work on a solution here. You know about these mineral rights matters and if you can, and will, that could be useful to gettin' at the bottom of this mess."

"Of course I will," Buck said with humility and sincerity.

"Good, then we'll join up with the posse and let you know how we do. And you do the same. If you hear of anything, go to the Double M and they'll find us," Micah finished.

As the huge front doors closed behind them, Paddy said, "I noticed ye didn't tell where the posse were headed."

"Exactly," Micah confirmed.

When they mounted their horses the moon was hidden but a faint bit of light shone through a break in the clouds. They headed for the MM and when they arrived, Abraham was waiting on the front porch.

"How many we got for the posse?" Micah asked the young man, to which Abraham held up six fingers.

CHAPTER SEVEN

ROCKY MOUNTAIN LAW

There was an old saying the real mountain men used to profess to the flatlanders that went something like this; *If the man ain't up for the mountains, then the boy best head for the hills.* It wasn't meant to be an insult. It was meant to make most think before they took on more than they could climb, so to speak.

Many a man was tested to failure in the Rocky Mountain range. The weather could change in minutes. The wild animals were always hungry and didn't like trespassers taking their food sources. The native Indians hated the white intruders trapping in their territory unless there were guns to trade. And getting lost wasn't chancy, it was probable. Winston Winchester Colt was thinking about all of those things as he followed the trail to the first cabin. He looked up to the tall, snow covered peaks before him and took a deep breath. The aspen trees made a rustling noise in the light wind and aspens swayed gently while the pines gave off a fresh, clean scent after having been watered by the rains. Winston lightly legged Thunder and they moved forward.

There were four kidnappers ahead of him, he figured, plus Marilyn Montgomery.

MARILYN WAS NOT A WILLING CAPTIVE, as the four men found out when they asked her to change clothes. They wanted her to strip in front of them. When one of the men neared her, she nearly scratched an eye out of its socket. Desiring money more than carnal pleasures, the leader, Ben

Franks, decided that if they were to get the best price then the goods had better be undamaged. Besides, there would be less chance anyone would follow them into the Rockies, he reasoned, if it was only money that had changed hands. Dead or damaged bodies make for relentless posses.

Marilyn had sized up all four of them. She knew that Ben was the leader because everyone waited to do what he said. He shouted orders when they got to camp, and in his haste they all revealed their names. She vowed never to forget them. Ben was lean, good looking with a small mustache, clean shaven and wore his gun low so the tip of the holster showed under his sheepskin coat.

The man who nearly lost the eye looked like a big mountain man with at least twenty five years of experience in the wilds. He was called Wolf. He even wore the face of a wolfskin hat with the tail trailing down his back. He was bundled in furs he had probably trapped himself, and he must have never bathed because he smelled like an animal. His pal, Bear, was similar looking only younger and skinnier and he had a bear claw necklace he wore proudly. It made noise when he walked.

The fourth one they called Stevie. He was a late teen aged kid and did the menial work at the orders of any of the other three. He was man sized and sturdy, but he didn't look like he should be in the mountains. He didn't have the confidence of the others. His blonde hair and blue eyes made him look innocent and childlike. The only thing that worried Marilyn was that he leered at her all the time, as though he had never been with a woman and wondered if this should be the first time. She didn't like the feeling she got from him, studying her constantly. The others, she reasoned, wanted the money. But Stevie, she wasn't so sure about. She was glad that she hadn't trimmed her finger nails lately. They were long and sharp.

Bear was the first to spot the hunters' cabin ahead on a knoll in the middle of a meadow. It was the perfect place to be in order to spot animals or humans that may approach. He held up his hand for the others to stop.

"Smoke," Bear announced, "means someone is in the cabin."

Bear and Wolf had the best hunters eyes to spot game, so Ben ordered,

53

"Bear, you and Wolf circle the meadow around the cabin and see if anyone is around. We'll ride directly towards the cabin."

Wolf was about a quarter mile from the cabin when he removed his Henry rifle and fired. Ben looked in his direction and saw a man running up a hillside, then stumble as if hit by a bullet. Then the man got up and limped into the trees.

"Damn you, Wolf," Ben whispered to himself, "I didn't tell ya ta kill nobody."

Ben, Stevie and Marilyn stopped out of pistol range of the cabin to see that the door was open. Ben dismounted and drew his 4 ¾" barrel Colt .45.

"Anyone in there?" he yelled towards the cabin, and the door swung closed. "Listen, we won't hurt you if you come out now."

A shotgun barrel emerged from a port in the door. Ben backed away.

"You just kilt my man, I reckon," came a woman's voice behind the door.

"No, just winged him, I think," Ben tried to assuage, "that damn fool wasn't supposed to hurt anyone. We'll find him and fix things up. Now put down that scatter gun and let's talk. We need to stay in the cabin for a day or so."

"How can I trust you?" the voice asked.

"Well, your options are to try to hold off four rifles and probably die, or share the cabin. Which is it?"

"I only see two men and a woman," she answered.

Ben stepped farther away. Stevie, still mounted, had moved closer to the cabin. Then the shotgun blasted at him. It wasn't buckshot at all. It was a ball and it hit Stevie in the left shoulder throwing him off his horse. The gun then swung back in the direction of Ben.

"Now they's only three of you," the woman behind the door screamed. "I gots lots 'o ammunition in here and more guns. You ain't comin' in 'til I see my ol' man."

As she was yelling, Ben noticed that Wolf was on the roof of the cabin. He had a blanket in his hand which he placed over the hole of the chimney. The smoke quickly began to waft out of the windows. After a minute the woman ran at Ben, choking but with her shotgun ready to fire. He quickly shot and hit her hand, causing her to drop the weapon. She didn't stop running but ran right by them, across the pasture and into a stream. Ben looked but couldn't see her. He then saw Stevie trying to stand up near his horse. His first priority was to help his nephew.

Seeing that Ben was distracted, Marilyn squeezed her horse firmly with her heels startling it into a run. Ben ran to his horse in order to pursue her when he saw Bear on his horse heading her off across the field. In the pandemonium, the two occupants of the cabin had escaped. Ben saw that two horses were corralled nearby, so he reasoned that they wouldn't get far. He did not like this new wrinkle, but he decided not to pursue them. They had tonight and tomorrow morning before anyone could reach them, and by that time they would all be gone.

WINSTON AND THUNDER RESTED. The rain had cleared and the half moon no longer lit the trail. It was the middle of the night and morning wasn't that far off. A warm fire and a cup of cowboy coffee helped. He didn't mind the gritty grounds because his insides were now warmer. He pulled his hat down over his face and closed his eyes and slept.

Without enough rest yet, Winston's eyes opened. Thunder had talked his nervous whinny. Winston pushed his hat up and shucked the blanket. Both Colts were in his hands. He squinted in the faint morning light. He must have slept a few hours, he thought. He heard a crackle of twigs.

He made out two figures in the dim misty light. They seemed to be holding on to one another. Winston rose up with guns trained on them. As they got closer he could see that the man had an old musket slung over his back. He was a scruffy man, but solidly built, and his woman wore the same style denims as he did. He had a coat on but she only had a shawl to keep her warm.

"Don' shoot," came a man's voice. "I done bin shot a'ready by ruffians up at da hunta's cabin. We mean no harm ta ya. He'a, ya kin have ma musket."

"Whoa, I don't want to hurt you," Winston reassured. "Matter o' fact, I'm chasin' someone up that way."

"I see'd 'em all," the woman said, shivering from the cold.

"Did they have a woman with them? She has red hair, and…"

"Yup, three men and that's her," answered the woman.

"I've been trailing what looked like five riders," Winston said.

"I kilt one o' 'em," she bragged. "Least 'a think a did. Fell offin 'is harse afta' I shot at 'im, he did."

"You gonna shoot us, mister," the man asked.

"Oh, sorry," Winston apologized holstering his guns. "The woman you saw was kidnapped. Do you know who Marilyn Montgomery is?"

"Heard o' her. Did some wurk at 'er spread once, but ne'er saw her in person. Paid real good, she did."

"What were you doing up there?" Winston asked.

"We bin a huntin' for elk before winter sets in. We got a place over yonder south of Sage Brush. Our boy is a watchin' the farm so's we could git some meat fer the winter. Best huntin' spot I ever found. Bin huntin' outta that cabin since I was a boy. Not fair them 'nappers run us out. Mountain law says we's all 'posed ta share, 'ceptin' maybe with the Indians, if ya ain't got nuthin' ta trade."

"Well, we've got a posse coming. We're going to get Miss Montgomery back," Winston informed the couple. "By the way, my name is Winston. Winston Colt."

"You one o' them Colt family members? You could be by tha looks o' them fancy guns and that fancy rig a yorn."

"Yessir, I am."

"Well, I'm right pleased to know ya, sir. I'm Horatio Wilfred Magillicuddy, but I go by Billy, 'cause they all call me Hillbilly for fun. But I don' mind as 'counta 'ahm proud o' being from the Ozarks. Dan'l Boone country. Oh, and this here is my dear waff, Eunice."

"Nice to meet you both. How badly are you hurt?"

"Well, I got nicked on the ear, but Eunice got her hand shot clear through. She needs to see a doctor," Billy said with concern.

"The posse should be here soon if you can wait. I'll leave you my coffee and some beef. Eunice can stay warm by the fire with my blanket," Winston offered.

"That's might' kind o' ya, sir," Billy thanked, "all take ya'll up on that offer, 'ceptin' I'm going back ta the cabin."

Winston thought that one over for a moment. The man probably wanted his possessions back, he reasoned. Actually, he thought, he'd feel more comfortable with a guide and the man did have a gun. Maybe he could save some valuable time by catching the kidnappers at the first hunters' cabin before they had a chance to move on to higher ground.

"Okay," Winston agreed, "let's go."

MICAH HAD SIX MEN WITH HIM. He knew them all to be dependable and good with their weapons. What he didn't know is if they would be able to rescue Marilyn before something bad happened to her. The money issue worried him, too, because he didn't understand it. He wondered why someone would want her mining rights so bad as to force a ransom. He also reckoned that Buck Krupp was the only man in the territory who could get that kind of money together, and that he also was invested in mining.

The tracks had been easy to follow up to the point where Winston had met up with the Magillicuddy couple. Eunice was sipping coffee by the campfire when they arrived. The posse wasted no time. They divided the stores from one of the pack mules and loaded them on the other two. They gave Eunice one of the mules to ride back to wait at the MM ranch. Then they moved out up the mountain. They were probably two hours behind Winston and Billy, who were double riding on Thunder. The extra weight would slow them down, so Micah figured they could catch up before they got to the cabin. He was wrong.

Billy jumped off Thunder when the cabin was in sight and said to Winston, "I'll circle around low under the grass so's they won't see me. You go to that stand of trees over there with your rifle and fire into the weenders. When they pokes their guns out, I'll get the first one with ol' Kentucky here. She's fifty caliber and ne'er misses."

Winston nodded and galloped out of sight to the trees that were about fifty yards from the cabin. He tied Thunder loosely to some brush so he could escape if there was trouble from man or animal. He could see Billy's musket above the grass. Billy was at the bottom of the knoll below the cabin behind a rock. Winston loaded some more rounds into his carbine and judged the distance to the first window. He took aim and let two bullets fly. The glass shattered.

A rifle barrel came out of the window. Then the valley roared as if a cannon had gone off. Billy's bullet flew true and the rifle in the window fell to the ground outside the cabin. Then Winston hit another window. But this time there was no response. He circled to the back of the cabin and shot again, and again there was no response. He noticed in the corral in back of the cabin that there were only two horses. Those he figured were probably Billy's stock. Winston recalled that Eunice had shot one of the kidnappers. They must have left him behind. Winston moved around and waved to Billy that he was going to close in. He ran to the front door and fired a shot through it. There was no sound after that. Billy was by now next to him. Billy crashed through the door and plowed over the table in the middle of the room. Winston set his rifle against the cabin and entered it with both Colts drawn and cocked. The only noise after that was the crackling of the fire. A young man lay dying on the floor.

"Ya'll done kilt me for the second time," Stevie moaned, now with the other shoulder nearly torn off by the big fifty ball.

"Where's the woman?" Winston ordered.

"Gone," the wounded man said. "And don't ask me no more questions 'cause they didn't tell me as they knowed you'd be a comin'."

Billy gathered himself and went over to the dying boy to check him for weapons. He was clean, even without a knife.

"Question is," Winston wondered aloud, "do we go after them or wait for the others."

"I don't mean to be no spoil sport, Mr. Colt," Billy stammered, "but this ain't 'zactly my fight. I got my stuff back and all an' ah' needs to tend to ma waff."

"I understand. But, can you tell me where they are likely to be headed?"

"Well, for one thing, they gonna be easy to foller. Snow fell day 'er two ago so's tracks' be everywhere. How's about I help ya fer a mile 'er so an' then a'll draw a map so' ya knows what ta look fer."

"That'll do. Then you can tell the others where I went."

Winston gathered supplies, took the map and lit out with Billy. In only a half hour or so he and Thunder were again on the trail; alone. It was midday and warmer. The trace of snow was beginning to melt. He quickened Thunder's step.

"Well, old friend," he said, "another adventure we can jaw about. Who's gonna believe we actually did all these things together?" Thunder snorted. "Yeah, big guy, I don't care either."

MICAH AND HIS POSSE ARRIVED at the first cabin about an hour behind Winston. When Micah discovered that Winston had gone on alone, he was worried. He did not know how capable this youngster was at dealing with criminals. He knew that being a good hand with a gun was not enough. It's one thing to shoot straight, but it's another to be able to get that first shot off before an ambush. And that's just how Winston was about to be tested. Micah and the posse trotted their horses after the trail Winston was following.

It wasn't more that five miles before Thunder started acting nervous. Winston had learned to trust his friend's instincts. They hesitated and covered themselves behind a stand of tall, thick pines. Thunder lifted his head to smell for danger. Then he nodded his head rapidly.

"Sure you're a human in horse clothes," Winston mumbled, as he withdrew his Winchester from its scabbard and looked around. He wasn't in a hurry at this point. He waited. He listened. Thunder stood absolutely still. He had done this routine before. He knew Winston as well as the man knew him. Harmony is what comes from wanted togetherness. Their act was well rehearsed and their song was well blended.

The sun was shining at just past high noon. Winston looked for a sign, then he thought he saw a flash of reflected light up ahead on the trail. He got off Thunder and moved around to another tree. The flash appeared again. Someone had a bead on him.

Winston drew one of his nickel plated Colts. He pulled off one of his spurs, looped the strap in the trigger guard and buckled it to a small branch nearby. As it hung there the sun caught it and reflected wildly in all directions. Winston led Thunder away, let him go and moved up the hill in the direction of the flash of light he has seen. Then he saw it flash again. As he moved forward he could see some movement. Then he saw what he knew was a nickled rifle barrel. He crept up quietly, muffled by the rustle of the pines in the breeze. Then a shot rang out. Winston took the opportunity to run at the shooter.

As he approached the man he lifted his rifle at him. The next step he took was on a two inch fallen pine bough which caused him to slip and fall on his elbows. His rifle fired, alerting the other man to his presence. The bushwhacker swung his big Henry around over Winston's head. Winston rolled over and down further. When he looked up the Henry was two inches from between his eyes. The man holding it was smiling, but with only one front tooth.

"Hi, there, boy. Don't move," Wolf calmly advised. "Anyone with ya?"

"Yeah," Winston conjured, "a few."

Wolf looked down the hill and still saw the pistol gleaming in the sunlight.

"Get up," Wolf ordered.

Winston slowly got up, rifle in hand. Wolf nodded for him to set it down, which he did. Wolf was looking between Winston and down the hill. He knew the man wouldn't shoot him because he'd be out of bargaining power if it came to that. His right hand was twitching and the Colt .45 was ready.

From behind them came a sudden loud sound like a roar. Wolf turned to see what it was and saw Thunder snorting as he raised up on his hind legs. His Henry was still trained on Winston. In that split second Winston drew his sidearm and fired hitting Wolf right where the tail connected to his wolf skin cap. The bullet exited out the top of his head taking flying fur with it, and the force of the .45 slug at point blank range lifted him slightly off the ground and then he flew face down into the mud.

Winston went over and grabbed Thunder by the nose and gave him a big kiss on his cheek. He led the horse back to collect his left holster pistol, reattached his spur and then mounted up and started down the trail again.

The posse had heard the shots echoing in the canyons. Micah knew he was getting close to catching up to Winston, he just hoped that the correct gunman was still alive when he did. Micah fired three shots from his pistol. Winston fired three shots back. But he kept riding ahead. He figured he'd get to the next cabin, scout out the situation and wait for the posse. He hoped that was the last surprise he'd get along the way.

CHAPTER EIGHT
DEAD AND ALIVE

———

Marilyn was made comfortable in the second hunters' cabin. It had three separate sleeping rooms besides the main living, eating and kitchen area. They kept her windows shuttered up from the outside, but she was at least left alone to her privacy. There were only two men who had arrived with her so she thought she may now have a chance for escape. That was a fleeting thought. When she was resting in her bedroom she heard more horses riding up and then she heard the loud clomping of at least a half dozen pairs of boots on the wooden floors. Voices confirmed that another group of men had joined them. She took a deep breath and cried. For the first time since her face was mangled, she cried. Then she slept.

A knock at her bedroom door awakened Marilyn. There was no light in the room. She couldn't see anything until the crack in the door allowed lantern light to filter in. A woman's head poked in.

"Miss Montgomery, the men want us to cook them up something," the woman half whispered.

Marilyn turned her head but didn't rise. Then she answered, "Fat chance. Tell 'em they can cook for me."

Ben Franks swung the door wide open and said, "It ain't a request. It's an order."

The tone of his voice made Marilyn weigh the alternative. She swung the blankets off her body, slid off the side of the bed and stood in the doorway to look into the living area. She then said to the woman, "What's your name?"

"Conchita," the Mexican woman answered.

"Get me outta here alive," she whispered to Conchita, "and you'll have a good job for life."

Conchita nodded, smiled and nudged Marilyn out the door. The men sitting around the table stopped what they were doing and stared at the classy redheaded woman before them.

"Mmmmm," one of the men moaned to taunt her, "I like that." He got off his chair and went over to her. She eyed him defiantly. He walked around her while the other men sat there absolutely quiet with anticipation. When he got around facing her again he grabbed her chin lightly. "I bet you're a real wild one," he chided. Then he moved his hand up the right side of her face and quickly moved the hair away that always covered it. He held it in a bunch in back of her head so that everyone could see her full face. She grabbed at his arm to move it away, but the man was too big and too strong. His entire body seemed to freeze. He couldn't move and she couldn't move him.

He could not control his eyes from staring at her right cheek. It was like when you look at someone who has a glass eye; you can't stop staring at it even though you know you shouldn't. Her cheek looked like a round hole had been filled in with a round piece of skin and all sewn together around the edges like the rim of a wrinkled volcano. Seeing it revealed the way it was, no one in the room even took a breath, except Bear.

"I see'd a trapper once had a scar like that," Bear announced, "caused by a wolverine what grabbed his face and wouldn't let go 'til he shot it through the jaw with his...er, pistol," he hesitated, scratched his beard then added, "is that what I heerd 'bout you, ma'am?"

"Take a good look, all of you," Marilyn spat, "Yes, that's what happened to me and by a no good just like you all here in this room. Go ahead, you jerk," she directed to the man holding her head, "take a good long look. Excite you?"

He let go and backed away, allowing her hair to fall back across her face.

"Now leave me alone, all of you. You'll all pay for what you've done one way or the other, and I'll be right there in front of you when you do." She turned towards the stove and joined Conchita's side. Marilyn took a deep breath to help whiten her face that had gotten as flushed as a prairie wildflower as much from ire as from embarrassment.

"I don't show my face to anybody," the female in her admitted to Conchita in a whisper.

"Don't matter, ma'am," Conchita consoled, feeling female kinship for the beleaguered woman, "you'll get through it."

Marilyn looked around with a scowl at the men. Then she saw it, in the hand of the man who had touched her. He was twirling it with his glove on. It was the same kind of pistol she saw in the cases that Buck had showed to everyone at dinner the other night; blue frame and barrel with a nickel silver cylinder.

"God help me," she thought, "I'm a dead woman."

"Alright," Franks woke them up, "I need three of you outside on watch. You over there, watch the back trail, the way you came in. You, there, watch the other trail and Bear, get up on the roof so's you can see all around. Both of you at the trails signal to Bear with a white cloth if you see anyone comin' up. Stay hidden in position though so you can get 'um from behind if there's trouble. Now we don't expect anyone is gonna follow us up here in time to do anything. Wolf is watching the trail. But, until we hear about the money, we're gonna watch our backs. Everyone get it?"

The group moaned agreement.

"And no one, I mean no one messes with the goods," Franks ordered, "that's our gold mine right there. Everyone got that?"

Again the men moaned agreement.

Winston saw the three men exit the cabin. One of them was coming towards where he was sitting on Thunder. He turned the horse and hid him behind a cropping of boulders. He pulled a small packet of oats out of his saddle bag and spread it on the long grass on the ground. He knew that would keep the stallion occupied for a bit. Then he climbed to the top of the rocks to see where the man was going to hide. From that vantage point he could see that another man was on the roof of the cabin and another was headed to what looked like an opening in the trees at the other end of the pasture. It must be a different trail from Sage Brush, he thought. He could see the man closest to him had taken up behind some rocks near where the trail opened on to the clearing.

It wasn't the same set up as the first cabin. This cabin was in a clearing but there were lots of trees around it. It was a higher altitude, so Winston reasoned that the trees would shelter the cabin and its occupants from the heavier weather. Also, the cabin was bigger than the first, meaning it probably had more provisions. It was the custom to leave a hunters' cabin with provisions for the next visitor. One never knew when it could occur to being trapped in these mountains without food. He could see the smoke billowing from the chimney. There were maybe a dozen horses tethered around the cabin. He assumed there were at least a half dozen more men in addition to the ones he had followed this far; minus one, of course.

The cowboy watching his trail rolled and lit up a smoke. Winston saw the flash of the sulfur then the puff of white smoke. The wind gave him away as well. The odor was distinct. The man would be distracted in his enjoyment and Winston decided to take advantage of the opportunity. He climbed higher until he was looking down on the smoker, who was by then looking at the ground and grinding the butt into the rock floor. Winston found a small boulder and dropped it on the man's head, crushing it.

"That was for Thunder," he mumbled to himself, "he prefers cigars." Then he propped the man up on the rock so it looked like he was still watching the trail. He could see the man on the roof was fighting the chimney smoke that seemed to follow wherever he went.

Smoke seemed to be the distraction of the day, Winston thought. "Huh," he wondered aloud, "smoke seems to be bad for their health."

Winston retreated back to where Thunder had just finished all of the oats. He gave him another handful, grabbed his binoculars, and got back up on the rock cropping so he could observe the cabin. He had reasoned that even if he had eliminated two of the kidnappers, trying to get six or eight armed men would be suicide. He sat on the rock watching for any changes when he saw a rider loping towards the cabin.

It was a big man, he could see with the naked eye. Raising the glasses to his eyes he couldn't keep the words from coming, "Damn him."

The sentry appeared to know the rider and had waved him by. As he did so and the rider passed, Winston saw the sentry begin to slump. The rider had already passed and did not see what had happened. The sentry then fell forward and crashed to the pine needled dirt under the trees. A Bowie knife protruded from his back. Winston's glasses followed the rider headed towards the cabin.

Unbeknownst to Winston, the knife thrower had emerged from behind a huge pine and approached the fallen man, putting his rifle barrel to the man's head. He kicked him to be sure there would be no counter attack. Then he pushed the knife in farther, twisted it around, then pulled it out. He wiped the man's blood on the man's own hide jacket.

"That's for Miss Marilyn," he spat at the body. He sheathed the knife and looked to the clearing where the man he had been following had ridden to the hunters' cabin he himself had visited many, many times. He reached down and stripped the dead man of his holster belt and strapped it on himself. He drew the pistol quickly, then spun it a few times to test the balance. "Needs two bullets," he said aloud. He took the cartridges from the belt and reloaded the pistol. Then he stepped over the man and looked at the cabin again. He saw Bear on the roof who was still fighting the smoke.

The rider rode directly to the front door of the cabin and dismounted. Bear saw him and waved. The man stormed through the front door.

Winston's jaw still was dropped from amazement. Out of the corner of his eye he saw movement. It was a man coming from where the rider had emerged out of the forest. He raised his glasses again and his jaw still didn't close. "Well, I'll be," he said.

Rocky Mountain was stomping across the clearing headed directly towards the cabin. Bear didn't see him coming, but Rocky wasn't exhibiting any stealth. When Rocky got fifty yards away he raised his Henry and fired one shot. Bear rolled off the roof to the front of the cabin. He limped inside holding his gun shot leg.

Winston stood up on the rocks and whistled as loud as he could and waved his arms. Rocky saw him and waved back. Windows broke out from inside the cabin. Bullets let fly in all directions. When Winston hit the ground he was greeted by Micah and the posse.

"I see ya waited for reinforcements," Micah said.

"I hope you don't mean Rocky, because he's headed towards the cabin," Winston answered. "And guess who just entered through the front door?"

"I'd guess it was Buck Krupp," Micah smiled.

"You're good at this," Winston added.

Rocky was walking straight at the cabin on the side with the chimney. There was only one window on that side. He was firing his Henry through the window until all the glass was broken out. No one could get a shot through it. When he got to the cabin he rested against the warmth of the chimney, out of any line of fire. He looked around and saw movement around the clearing. He guessed it was Winston, Micah and the posse; and Abraham. He heard a crackling sound and looked up. The chimney was spouting steam instead of smoke from the fire being put out from inside.

The firing stopped from inside the cabin then a voice boomed, "The woman is dead if you all don't leave."

Being closest Rocky decided to answer, "If you harm that woman none of you will ever see the night fall."

There was a long silence. The front door opened. Buck Krupp exited with his hands up.

"Buck," Micah shouted, "what's this all about?"

"I heard about the gun used to slap Marilyn's foreman, Rocky. There is only one man carry's a weapon like that. It's my brother. I came here to talk him out of going through with this whole mess."

"Seems strange you knowing exactly where he was goin', if you're sayin' you have nothin' to do with all this," Micah challenged.

"We hunt up here every year, like everyone else. I got a message that said he was being held captive here. I don't think he's a part of any scheme. I think he's here against his will."

A pistol popped out of the window near Rocky. He drew the Bowie knife and chopped it over the man's wrist. The pistol dropped to the ground.

The cabin was now surrounded by the posse. All weapons were trained on it. Micah rose up to be in sight of Buck. He knew he was vulnerable to a rifle shot, but his hunch was that the men inside would probably try to negotiate themselves a deal.

"Look, Buck, tell everyone inside to let Marilyn go. If you do, it'll go better on all of them at the trial," Micah offered.

"I don't think so," Franks yelled, as he exited the door. "We've got ten men inside, lots of firepower and we have the woman. You ain't gonna risk hittin' her by firing on us. Now we're gonna move out, and if you follow, we'll cut something off of her for every man we see on our trail. Do you understand that, marshal?"

Rocky froze in thought. Then he retreated back into the trees. Being a master scout and tracker, he knew his day would come to rescue Marilyn. If this wasn't it, then he'd win on another day.

Franks went back into the house, leaving Buck still standing in front. Then all hell broke loose. Rifle and pistol fire emanated from every window of the cabin. The posse did not return fire; just as the outlaw had predicted. Then with the two women in amongst a circle of the eight men, they all exited the cabin together. All that Micah and his posse could do was watch, duck, and wait. The outlaws set the women on two mules, then they all mounted up and rode west, up towards a higher elevation. Micah figured they were headed to another cabin.

Micah and Winston walked up to Buck Krupp.

"They want the $250,000 in two days or they'll kill her," Buck said. "And truthfully, I have nothing to do with this mess. My brother organized it. Supposedly on behalf of my family, I am very ashamed. My family has nothing to do with this. It's all him and some other scallywags."

"We'll see about that later," Micah said, "and so, where are your new pistols?"

"They should be back at the ranch by tomorrow. It'll prove I had nothing to do with this."

"How?" Winston added.

"You'll see," Buck insisted, "you'll see."

"We need a plan," Micah stated, "so let's go inside and make one.

Buck, I'm gonna send you back to Sage Brush under arrest. You've got to wait for me at the jail. Agreed?"

"Agreed," the big man affirmed.

Micah signaled for one of his posse and Buck and he rode away down the trail.

"They're gonna always have someone scouting out behind to see if we're following," Winton noted as he sipped coffee at the table across from Micah.

"Yeah, I know," Micah agreed.

"Sir, may I say something?" Abraham chimed to a nod from the marshal. "My father went back into the woods. He's already trailing them. He used to be a scout for the U.S.Army. He told me how he would track raiding parties and pick off outlaws one at a time, quietly. I think that's what he will do. And I know where they're headed. There's only one hunters' lodge they could go to where they all would be able to breathe right. The others are too high and the snow would pack them in for the winter."

"Good point, Micah," Winston said. "Here's what I think. I'll take Abraham with me and one other man. It'll probably be better for Marilyn if we let Rocky do what he does best. Abe, do you know any short cuts to the other cabin?"

"Sure do," Abe said enthusiastically, appreciating the others' giving him equal importance in spite of him being younger.

"Okay," Micah agreed. "I need to head off this ransom business. Buck is the only one who would know the source. His brother, Manfred, isn't the smart one in the family and could never do this alone. Anyway, you men go ahead. Be careful and send word back if anything changes. I'm gonna telegraph all the other jurisdictions to watch for anything suspicious. God speed, gentlemen."

Abraham guessed it would be a full day's ride to the higher cabin. It was now late afternoon and would soon be dark. It was beginning to mist again, but it wasn't extremely cold. The moon was rising early so there was still some light, but not great for narrow trails. Winston opted to stay the night in the cabin for the safety of all of them, including the horses.

Rocky Mountain, on foot, was following the outlaws.

ROCKY KNEW THE TRAIL WELL. He and his son had been along it at least ten times in the last five years. It was slow moving on horseback because it was mostly rock, and when wet very slippery. He knew the men he was following would have to camp somewhere in the night and he knew the most likely place would be by a small lake. Rocky took the shortcut; an elk trail.

When the train of horses was within sight of the lake it was pretty dark. The moon did light the mist enough to see the trail. Rocky was hidden in the darkness of a rock crevice as the horses passed him. He smelled Marilyn's perfume before she passed him. He was happy she was still safe but he did not have the opportunity to alert her that he was near. He waited until the last horse approached and then with Bowie knife in hand, his arm jutted out and nearly decapitated the outlaw, whose body slumped in its saddle but did not fall off. Now he figured there were only seven opponents.

"We'll set up camp here," Franks commanded of the group. He looked around to scope out the area and the last horse passed him on its way to the lake.

The horse entered the lake and dipped its tongue in the water for a drink. The rider fell off into the water. Franks and another man dismounted and pulled him out. They immediately noticed there was blood covering the man's clothing. His head fell lifelessly all the way over to his shoulder. They dragged him away from the others, drew their guns and tried to look into the darkness. They saw nothing.

"Think we're being followed?" Manfred whispered, now joining Franks' side.

"Of course not, he cut his own head off...you idiot," Franks spat back, "but probably only one man. Maybe an Indian. They don't like us up here sometimes. Let's form a circle around the campfire and get close to the lake. We'll each take an hour watch."

"Could be a critter, too," Bear offered, matter of factly.

Everyone looked at each other. It was getting spooky and their faces showed it. Something made a sound in the lake. It sounded like something had fallen from the sky. They huddled closer to the fire. A loud growl was heard in the distance. Then the call of wolves echoed through the trees and across the lake. Hands were on guns. Rocky Mountain smiled at the fear he saw on the fire lighted faces. He saw Marilyn against a rock, sheltered from the cold, but inaccessible. She looked up as if feeling a friendly presence. She couldn't see anything in the darkness, but she smiled anyway.

"It's going to be a long night for y'all," Rocky whispered to himself as he met her stare, that while she did not know it, was directly into his eyes.

The clouds now covered any light from moon or stars. Except for the low embers of the fire, the camp was completely dark. The men couldn't even see the trees around the lake. The air was colder now. It was crisp. Their steam from warm breath was getting thicker. Each inhalation of air seemed colder. Everyone knew that the temperature could change in these mountains without warning. And then the snow started to fall. It came down in large billowy flakes. Quickly a blanket of white covered the campsite.

"You, Chip," Franks ordered, "go get some more firewood. We're gonna need it. Take your buddy, there, with you. Get some big pieces if you can find 'em. One of you pick up wood and the other stand guard and watch for that Indian."

Chip and his friend rose up with their wool serapes wrapped over their heads. Chip grabbed a small burning twig for light. They had red kerchiefs around their mouths. No one could see the frowns on their faces, and they were not happy with their duty. The other five men huddled close to the fire and drew their guns under their blankets. Rocky saw the small armada and decided that he would even the odds a bit more.

The two men headed into the forest by the trail.

"I think I see'd a felled tree afore we entered the clearin'," Chip said to Cal, his buddy. "There'll be some cracked branches we can get quick."

Both men were bundled like experienced cowboys are who have done saddle time in cold weather. Rocky thought he should be a little less bold this time.

"Here's one that'll burn fer a while," Cal said to Chip, bending over to pick the broken limb up by himself. When he rose up he heard a cracking of smaller twigs. He dropped the branch and grabbed at his gun under his coat but then saw that it was nothing but Cal lighting another dry limb for more light. The snow was still falling slowly, but it was covering everything like sheets of fluffy cotton.

Cal planted the new flare in the ground and began picking up wood, as did Chip. When they both had their arms filled they turned again towards the lake. They put their backs together and Cal walked backwards. The fading flare provided little light but they could see a reflection ahead from the campfire. Chip slipped on the fresh, wet snow and fell on his butt causing Cal to fall on top of him. Chip's face was buried in cold snow. Cal was spread eagle across his back.

Cal looked up and saw a huge furry creature looming over him and he moaned in a gravely, frightened voice, "Bear!"

From out of the bearskin coat came a huge clawed sleeve that swiped down Cal's face, tearing away eyes, nose and mouth. He wasn't dead, but he wished it would come soon. The pain was excruciating and he was able to express it in a shrill scream that echoed off the snowflakes and across the lake. Footsteps were pounding towards them until Franks, rifle in hand, stopped a few yards away from the scene. He raised the weapon and fired, but it was too late. What appeared to be a bear was hidden among the trees already.

Behind a large pine Rocky shook the snow off his bearskin coat while still able to see Franks lower the rifle. "Down to six," he whispered.

ABRAHAM HAD THE HORSES saddled by the time Winston exited the cabin with a cup of mountain-made coffee in his hand. He nodded and smiled at the lad. The other man with them, Harry Cogsdell, was a farmer. He was neatly dressed in black everything except his heavy sheepskin coat. They had talked during the evening and Winston learned that the man didn't volunteer information. It had to be dragged out of him. The most important thing he learned, however, was that Harry carried a German made Schutzen rifle used for either long range shooting competitions, or by military trained snipers. It had a new technology telescope sight that he allowed Winston to gander through. The pine cones on the trees a mile away seemed easy targets. Winston learned early from an uncle who fought in many different wars never to underestimate a man by his demeanor. He often reminded Winton that a man who does not brag is probably the most dangerous. He was glad to know Harry Cogsdell as a new friend.

At the cabin, the sky was clear when they left. They arrived at the lake at about noon and saw the tracks in the snow that had fallen all night. While still cold, the sun showed through the clouds a might, and enough to mark the beauty around them. The campfire was long dead and there was a heap by the lake covered in a blanket. Harry dismounted his horse and pulled the blanket off. Abraham gasped at the sight of the two mangled men. He vomited.

"Rocky Mountain," Harry whispered to Winston. "Don't tell the boy."

"Abe, get a grip," Winston said, "you're a man now and your dad will need us soon. Take us the shortest route."

Composing himself, Abraham led the posse up the trail then took a fork nearer the lake. He knew his father was formidable, but he had never seen how much. He knew that his father had a deep affection for Miss Montgomery, but he never knew that would evolve to this kind of revenge. He wasn't sure if he should respect or fear his father now. He forged ahead as the scout anyway. Ironic, he thought, doing what his father used to do for a living. He also wondered if he would be capable of such acts if called upon. What he could not know, was that his time may surely come.

As the posse headed up to higher altitudes, Rocky followed the outlaws. All three parties were converging to the same point. Rocky arrived to the third cabin first.

The cabin built of heavy logs was like a fort against the weather. It was large enough that it was more lodge than cabin. It had one large greatroom with no extra bedrooms, a few small windows, a high roof, and two fireplaces. There was a coal bin and a stacked woodpile. Rocky knew it well. He had actually taken rich hunters to the site on occasion. It was stocked with canned food and jerky because the hunters paid extra not to be stranded without provisions. There was also a barn not far from the lodge where a dozen horses could be kept. It, too, was stocked with provisions and extra supplies for horses and men. While the barn was at the foot of a boulder pile, the lodge was built on the top of it. It was situated that way so the game could be seen in all 360 degrees. That was good for hunters in the lodge, but bad for potential attackers, like Rocky.

He stood in a dark crevice below the lodge surveying the terrain. Smoke was coming from both of the chimneys. He took a piece of jerky from his pocket and chewed it. He then knew his next move.

There were two trails up the rocks to the lodge. Both were initially lined by trees that thinned to bare rock at the top. No tree was high enough to block the view from the lodge. It was a perfect fortress.

A cloud hung over the lodge as though the chimneys were the bottoms of funnels of tornados. The literal connection of the smoke to the cloud was eerie. It roiled and boiled. Then the cloud lowered to cover the lodge. It was loaded with heavy iced rain. The lodge was being covered in ice as the sun shone everywhere else around the mountains surrounding the basin below.

Rocky moved in. He dropped the heavy bear coat and with rifle in hand and pistol belted tightly around his waist he ran like a warrior up the front road. He knew he would not be seen from above.

When Rocky reached the porch that circled the lodge he slipped on the ice that had stuck to the steps. When he fell, the rifle dropped and wedged between rocks about twenty feet away. The noise alerted a guard who looked downward through the misty iced fog and saw the intruder on his back. The man drew his pistol and fired at Rocky. The shot grazed Rocky's boot, tearing a notch near his big toe.

"Bastard," Rocky screamed as he rolled over and got to his knees. He drew the Russian .44 from its holster and clipped off two rounds that hit the guard in the neck and right between the eyes.

The dead man slammed against the lodge wall then ricocheted forward and fell off the porch, and then slid on the ice right past Rocky. Another man exited a nearby door with a rifle. Rocky had four more rounds left so he let another bullet fly but it more fizzled than exploded out of the barrel. The misfire hit the man's chest but he did not fall from the powerless bullet. He raised his rifle and fired just as Rocky rolled to his right. The bullet missed but as Rocky looked up he saw the odds change. Three more men exited with rifles. The fog was flowing around all of them and getting thicker, colder and icier. Rocky slid down the path and managed to grab his Henry on the way as his momentum on the ice took him out of view through the fog. Bullets bounced all around him but none hit him. Well, he thought, at least he eliminated another of them.

Rocky stopped sliding between two large pines. It hurt. As he wallowed in the pain he heard horse hooves clunking and slipping. The fog blew by and opened his view to the barn. Marilyn Montgomery was being assisted off her horse. The six men around her looked tired, but mean. Rocky decided to stay in the fog and wait for the next opportunity. The men in the lodge now knew he was there and they weren't safe. In his mind Rocky was confident that he would win this war. He wondered when reinforcements would arrive. He was by experience, after all, a soldier and a lawman. He was used to the regimental life. Battles can be won alone, he had learned, but wars are won with regiments.

CHAPTER NINE
THE LODGE AND THE LADY

Marilyn wasn't happy that there was not a separate bedroom for her in the lodge. It was a hunting lodge, as she was told, not a resort. They had rigged up a blanket in a corner of the room to give her some privacy, but with a dozen men now inside she knew there would be little if any chance to escape. She hated being looked at anyway, especially by people she hated.

"Alright, everyone, I got to a say a piece here," Ben Franks announced.

The men gathered around except for the two guards walking the porch that surrounded the lodge. Franks took off his jacket, scarf, gloves and hat and laid them down on his bunk. Marilyn was watching him closely. He was a handsome man and had been normally quiet but mean looking. He had a glazed look in his blue eyes that made him look crazed. But she knew he was very savvy. She noted that his pistol was apparent in its buscadero holster, which was studded with silver and turquoise. He constantly fiddled with the weapon by lifting and dropping it into the holster. She figured the reason he hadn't flirted with her was because he loved that gun more than any woman. She was correct. It had never let him down.

"This little dinner party is havin' a few hiccups. We didn't really think anyone would find us this fast, so we need to be more careful. It really don't matter none that they know where we are 'cause they don't want to hurt our goods over there." That said, the group of men all looked over at Marilyn, who made no expression whatsoever. "Miss Montgomery is worth a quarter of million dollars to us. You all know your shares and you now get a bigger share because three are dead. We think it's an injun doin' it, but we don't know fer sure. Keep an eye out. Now, the big boss of this operation is gonna tell ya what the status is on our gettin' paid."

Manfred Krupp stood up before the group. He was a big man, thick and tall like his brother, but he did not have the power, the authority, or the mettle to give off the same air of confidence. In short, he did not have charisma.

Some men just seem to feel comfortable in command. Manfred did not emit that feeling. However, they all knew he could adeptly use the fancy Colt pistol he carried. Its blue frame and a well worn and powder stained nickel cylinder was unique but it had been made from parts of two guns. It was not a factory original. Oddly, the trigger guard had been heated and stretched to fit his gloved hand because he seldom was ever seen without a gauntleted hand. His family and its reputation were well known for its money and skill with weapons. The men in the room listened intently to hear when they could expect to be paid more than three years wages each for this effort.

"Gentlemen," Manfred began, "so far everything is going well. My brother, Buck, confirmed that my sources have made the offer we wanted. However, Buck is not a part of this deal, so we cannot expect any help from him. It is up to us now...me, actually. I have the papers for the lady to sign all nice and legal...well, sort of."

Bear stood up in the middle of the room and asked, "Can I say sumpn' here, boss?"

Manfred looked around, not liking the prospect of questions at this point, then nodded at Bear.

"Now, I may look like a big stump of unwashed mountain man, but I did get some learnin' when I was young. Maybe not as much as your fancy yuro-peen schoolin', Mr. Krupp, or your fancy east coast college there, Ben, but ya learn a lot livin' out here alone in the mountains. Ya get a kinda, well, common sense logic, ya might say. Ya gotta outthink bears and wolves and big cats that have been huntin' this territory since God created it. The only thing that makes us even close to equal to the critters out here is our brains, and of course...bullets and blades. So, don't take offense or nothin', but it came to me that maybe this whole scam ain't very likely to play out like ya planned."

There was movement in the room; the shuffling of uneasy feet and men leaning in to hear what Bear had to say, which caused Ben Franks to say, "Spit it out, Bear."

"Okay, it's like this. How is this lady gonna get a quarter million dollars to us if she's here? Ain't no one gonna loan it to her or pay that kind of money without some kind of payback."

Manfred stood up like a proud schoolboy all puffed with pride that he knew the answer, then said, "I can tell you it's all been planned out. This saddlebag I have here contains papers to sell the mineral rights at the Double M ranch. I have the buyer ready to give the money for the rights. All Miss Montgomery over there has to do is sign the papers."

"Well, I don't mean ta argue with ya, Mr. Krupp, but don't ya need a witness for them kinda things?" Bear added.

"The witness is outside right now. He just doesn't know yet that he's going to sign the papers," Manfred answered.

The men stirred again.

"Trust me," Manfred said, "I planned that, too. That ain't no Indian following us! It will be a willful sale, no duress. The lady has a ransom to pay, so she's selling her rights to a legitimate buyer to get the money."

"What's that mean, no dress?" one of the cowboys asked, scratching his head. "Looks like she's got a dress on ta my way o' seein' thangs."

"Doo-ress, not dress," Ben chimed in, "means someone is forced to do something for fear of something else happening to them."

"So, you all are sayin' this here lady ain't feared fer her laff, or nuthin' lack thet?" the cowboy astutely pointed out.

"Let me deal with that, Ben," Manfred interrupted. "In the first place, you have to trust us. You've been paid some money up front already. All I can say is that we have everything worked out and we will get the money, and you all will be paid. And that's all we're going to say on the matter. This is not up for a vote. You've been hired to do a job...period." He hesitated for a moment then added, "Everyone understand?" The men grunted agreement. "Good, then you each have your duties so do them."

Manfred motioned for Franks to join him outside. They left out the front door and into the ante-room that buffered the outside cold from stealing the warm comfort of the lodge.

"So far the plan is working," Franks said, "that injun story I made up seems to have worked."

"Rocky Mountain has killed three of your men already. I didn't consider that, actually. Brother Buck led him right to us, just as planned. I also didn't think a posse would be so quick to follow, but it doesn't matter. The sale will be legal anyway. The buyer has no idea this is a kidnapping for ransom, so signed and witnessed deeds and bills of sale mean everything out here. There can be no challenge," he said, re-entering the main hall, "besides, I've got some insurance planned."

"Yeah, what's that mean?" another confused cowboy pondered aloud.

Manfred rolled his eyes and smirked then rebuked, "That's none of your concern. You must trust me on this."

"We all here done trusted ya' a bit much a'ready," another commented.

"Yeah, and so did the half dozen or so of our comrades who ain't here no more to get their shares," another piped in.

"Whoa, whoa, here men," Ben chimed in, "we don't need a mutiny right now. Manfred, I think you should try explaining a bit about your...*insurance.*"

"Okay, okay. I sold the mineral rights for three hundred and seventy five thousand dollars. When the deed gets delivered to the buyer, we get the cash. A deposit will be made to her bank in the amount of one hundred twenty five thousand dollars just to show she received actual money in the transaction. We keep the rest to split, but no one is ever going to know how she spent what we got. It won't matter. She could have used it for anything, including to buy something else." He stopped smiling ear to ear. "So, the ransom idea was a diversion."

"Huh," someone said, as the cowboys seemed to be scratching their heads in unified confusion.

Everyone in the room was then quiet. They only heard the faint whistling of the wind against the building until they heard a loud cracking sound. Then they heard what sounded like a thump on the porch. Ben drew his pistol and looked down the porch to see that a man was standing holding his heart, and blood pouring over him.

"Sharpshooter," Ben yelled to Manfred, and then Ben ran back towards the door. A bullet ripped at the spot he had just left. The other man on the porch followed them.

"You'd better get this deal together before we lose all the men or have to kill the meal ticket," Ben snapped at Manfred.

From where he had moved to better see, Rocky saw Franks hustle back inside the lodge. This wasn't going to be easy he thought.

Winston and Abraham came through a thick stand of pines into a small meadow. Rocky was sitting on a rock above them. He whistled. Both of the Colt .45's from Winston's holsters were instantly cocked and pointed directly at the smiling tracker. Just as quickly they were spun back into the holsters.

Abraham's tears moved Rocky. He loved his loyal son. If only his mother was still alive to as well be proud of their son, he often thought.

Rocky apprised them of the situation. Winston said they had a sharpshooter with the group. When he described Harry's rifle, Rocky knew the weapon and the man that owned it.

"I've seen him hit a ram from a thousand yards," Rocky said, "and I just saw what old Harry can do again. He got another one of them. I've taken care of three others. But they still have a slew of them up there."

Winston pointed up the mountain across from the lodge. They saw a moving dot. It was Harry getting in position.

Rocky reported that there were four men guarding the barn and horses. They were heavily armed with shotguns and were well hidden. Any direct attack could cause a loss of one of the posse he felt. And, he reasoned, it was too cold to burn them out. The wood was wet.

"I think Harry will keep them all in the lodge building," Rocky said, "so we need to figure how to get Miss M out without them hurting her."

"You know about the ransom note?" Winston interjected.

"No."

"Someone wants a quarter million dollars for her."

"What?"

"According to Micah, the only way for her to get it is to sell the mineral rights to the ranch. He heard that from Buck Krupp."

"Well, they've got Manfred Krupp up there with them. I'm not sure if he's with 'em or against 'em. I wonder if he has something to do with all this," Rocky pondered, and then his face turned very dark and broodingly sullen.

"I wonder if Micah knows that?" Winston asked.

"I don't want to talk about it," Rocky said through gritted teeth. He looked towards his son, Abraham, who had been quietly and respectfully awaiting instructions. Rocky tried to smile but it was difficult. Rocky Mountain was not a happy man, and it showed.

"I think we need to deal with the barn," Winston suggested, to change the subject.

"Okay, okay," Rocky agreed, seeming to somewhat snap out of his mood.

"This is what I suggest," Winston started, "you go around the back and take this with you. It's a present from Micah." He handed Rocky two sticks of dynamite.

"Micah's fire we call that," Rocky said. "He loves evening odds with it."

"You've got two throws so toss the first one on the roof in the back so it blows down into the barn. If you don't hear me fire my pistols, then you've got to throw the other one. Give it ten, fifteen seconds to quiet down before throwing the second one. The four men will have to run out the front. I'll take care of them."

"Mr. Colt, what about me," Abe asked.

"You stay behind the trees and hold the horses. If I get shot, you ride back and tell Micah," Winston instructed. "Your dad can take care of himself with Harry up there to help.

"Yes, sir," Abe agreed.

"They've got shotguns in there so they won't be in your range until they get about 20 feet out the door," Rocky advised.

Winston nodded as Rocky made his way to the back of the barn. He climbed some rocks in the back of the barn and leaned his .50 caliber rifle against a tree. The back hay door at the second level was open. "This is gonna be easy," he laughed to himself.

Taking a sulfur tipped wooden stove match from his shirt pocket he ran it up the back of his Levi's. It crackled as it began to light. The flame sputtered and plumed as he put the dynamite's short fuse next to the fire. The fuse sparkled as the flame began its run down to the stick. He held it for five seconds then tossed it into the barn.

The boom echoed off the stone walls of the Rocky Mountain range magnifying the sound a thousand times. Rocky knew that it would be more than fifteen seconds before the noise quieted and he could toss the second one.

Four men exited at the same time. Every one of them had a double barreled stage coach shotgun and all eight barrels blasted at the same time. The pellets fell within inches of where Winston was standing at dead center to the doorway. This all happened within the time it takes for a heart to beat.

When the shotguns were tossed the men drew their pistols. Winston drew his right Colt, thumb cocked it then fired, felling the first man on his far right. Then he ran his hand over the top of the pistol allowing the thumb to catch and cock the fallen hammer while keeping his trigger finger squeezed tight. When his thumb passed over the now cocked hammer it dropped which let loose a .45 slug that caught the second man square in the heart. His index and middle fingers caught the hammer twice more to get the now closer third man twice in the chest. As the fourth man raised his pistol, Winston's ring finger then the little finger pulled the hammer back to let loose the final two rounds which made a close grouping in the man's stomach. All four men were on the ground, lifeless. Winston twirled his Colt .45 into its holster and drew the left one, cocked and ready. He walked toward the fallen men.

Rocky had not heard the sound of the bullets because his ears were still ringing. He lit and threw the second stick of dynamite into the now damaged barn anyway. Twelve horses ran out of the barn. The blast had knocked Winston flat on his back. His pistol was three feet away on the ground. He looked up through the haze of hay and smoke. A man emerged with a shotgun raised and pointed directly at him.

The first shot from the scatter gun covered him in pellets. He closed his eyes while trying to roll to his pistol. Then he heard a loud rifle shot from behind him. He looked up and saw Abraham Mountain with a rifle at his shoulder. Winston looked towards the barn to see his assailant fall to his knees and die. Instinctively, the boy racked another round into the chamber.

Rocky emerged from behind the barn. He saw the scene and knew what had happened. There wasn't much to say. The boy had been in a life or death situation and had done the right thing. Rocky had hoped his son would never have to see a man killed, let alone kill one. As Rocky had learned, life in the Rockies is half full of hope and half full of tragedy. Sooner or later tragedy finds you. It had just found his son.

"My fault, son," Rocky apologetically directed at Abe, "I miscounted. There was one inside I didn't see. I wish you hadn't had to do that, but since you did, it was the right thing to do."

Abe was crying. He'd never shot a man before. Winston and Rocky left him alone to reason what he had done, as the man he had become.

The men inside the lodge had lifted the interior window shutters to see what was going on down the hill. They had seen the barn blast, the guards shot, and their horses run off. Ben Franks did not need a mutiny right now and Manfred was pacing the wooden floor. The two fireplaces crackled with fiercely burning logs as the sap popped and flames lit the room.

"Sounds like the shining knights are here to save me," Marilyn laughed. "You'll never get away with this."

Manfred approached her and lifted her by her arm over to a window. She looked out and saw that the snow was falling very hard and piling up fast.

"We are provisioned to stay the winter," he said to her, "but they are not."

Marilyn Montgomery's heart sank.

"Are you ready to make a deal," Manfred asked of Marilyn.

"Just kill me now you cheap pig" she spat.

"Okay, you die, Rocky dies and your son, Abraham, dies," he answered with a wide, Cheshire cat smile.

She froze.

CHAPTER TEN

THE LADY DECIDES

Micah had known Buck Krupp since they both moved to the territory twenty years earlier. He had never known the man to lie to him.

"I don't know if my brother is being blackmailed, held hostage, or is a part of this deal," Buck confessed, "but I want nothing evil to happen to Marilyn."

"I believe you, Buck," Micah played, "but I need to know more."

The men were sitting in the intimidating confines of the law man's small office located in the heart of town. There was no one else in the room that was dimly lit by one kerosene lantern. Buck didn't like small spaces. His home attested to that. The seasoned lawman that he was, Micah observed the man's discomfort and intended to take full advantage of it.

"You've got to tell me the truth, Buck," Micah drilled also with his eyes, "and the whole story. Now, I know you and Marilyn had some trouble long ago, but you need to tie these things together for me. We need to get her back, safe."

"I know," Buck pouted almost like a child, "I don't want anything to happen to her either. I've been thinking on the whole thing. Brother Manfred has done a terrible thing. He was always the black sheep. Always in trouble and wanted the easy path. Very contrary to the Krupp way. Shameful, in fact."

"Well, then why not start from the beginning."

"The beginning…yes…the beginning." Buck took a deep long breath. "Well, I guess I've always been in love with Marilyn. From the first day I laid eyes on her she made my heart beat faster. That red hair, the piercing eyes, the perfect features, the way she carries herself with confidence and her straight honest manner all formed the perfect package for me. Trouble was, she never felt the same for me. Ah, and back then, back ten or twelve years ago I attracted a lot of ladies, and not just for my money. You remember, don't you, Sheriff?"

"Yes, I do," Micah confirmed, "you coulda had yer pick back in the day."

"Unfortunately for me, I picked Marilyn. She was just getting her herds formed; cattle and horses. She was just starting to make it on her own, with the help of Rocky Mountain. What a name. I hated him. Not because of his color, no, I've had many employees like him and good ones, too. Nope, it was because of his confidence. He had no money but he just had a swagger about him. He didn't need money to make him the man he was. He was a seasoned all around man. He'd done it all and it was like he didn't need to prove who or what he was to anyone."

"Maybe the word is prideful?" Micah suggested.

"Good choice, yes. She, I mean Marilyn, always treated him with respect; equally. She seemed to have a certain liking for him that went beyond just friendship or employee. I read too much into that, I guess, and got jealous. Then one night I was bringing her home from dinner in town. I'd had too much to drink. When my carriage pulled up to the house I got out and went to the other side. I didn't see that Rocky was sitting on the porch in the darkness. When I lifted Marilyn down from the carriage I hugged her against my body. She smelled so sweet of the perfume I had given her from my country from the city of Cologne. The best of the best. I was intoxicated with everything about her. I kissed her hard, too hard I guess. She started fighting. Then I felt someone grab me from behind. I instinctively turned and drew my pistol. As I turned the gun went off. That's when the tragedy happened."

"How come I never heard any of this before?" Micah asked.

"I'll tell you. Well, the bullet went in Marilyn's mouth and out her right cheek. The shock of what I saw made me go limp. I dropped the gun and fell to my knees. Rocky caught Marilyn before she fell to the ground. As he carried her up the stairs he told me to go get the doctor, but not to say how it happened. Why he did that I still don't know, but I went to town and sent the doctor to them."

"So, it was tragic, but an accident," Micah judged.

"I guess. I didn't see her for over a year. She never came to town. But Rocky Mountain did, once a month. About a year after the accident he started bringing a baby in to see the doctor. I knew whose baby it was; his and Marilyn's. But I didn't say anything. It was quid pro quo."

"Kinda like, your guilt as a trade off for discretion, eh?" Micah nodded.

"Maybe that's one way to explain jealousy and stupidity on my part. The problem is, I told Manfred the story a few months ago when we were both drunk and arguing."

"What difference would that make?"

"I had vowed to myself to never allow my jealousy to lower my integrity again, but I did. Manfred came to me the next week with a plan to blackmail Marilyn with that information. He had wanted to make a deal of his own to prove he was a Krupp of substance. He had found a mining company that wanted mineral rights in our area and he figured he could get them from Marilyn if he could get her to sell them to him. When she wouldn't hear of it, he decided to kidnap her for ransom."

"What's that got to do with her supposedly having a baby?"

"Marilyn has never admitted or let anyone know that Abraham Mountain is her son. Manfred intends to use that to convince her to sign away the rights. He thinks she would be devastated if anyone knew she and Rocky were Abe's parents."

"Harrumph," Micah blurted. "If that were true, none of us who knows her would care."

"Are you sure?"

"I'm sure. If you had really loved her you'd be, too."

Buck hung his head. He knew that the sheriff was correct.

CHAPTER ELEVEN
AND THEN ALONG CAME THUNDER

Marilyn seethed as she just took in the threat Manfred had made to kill all that was dear to her. But to kill her son? That was down right incomprehensible.

"I'm gonna kill that black devil and your devil child, too," Manfred reaffirmed.

"Why would you want to do that?" Marilyn asked unfettered.

"You and your uppity attitude. You should have married Buck when you had the chance. He would have elevated your station in life," Manfred bragged.

Except for the German's diatribe, the room was as quiet as the snow falling outside.

"Elevated?" Marilyn's goat was got, "How the hell is my station elevated when that bastard brother of yours did this to me?"

She lifted her red mane from the right side of her face.

There was a gasp in unison.

The men in the room may have been led astray by the evil of the greed of this caper, but they all had been suckled by mothers who fought for them to live in this harsh frontier. They respected the sanctity of the women of the West. They knew that it was important for men to be among other dependable men in danger and uncertainty, but there was something sacred about the women who stood right there with them in the harshest of times. Those women were special, and to the men in that room they could see that Marilyn Montgomery was one of those who fit the description.

Manfred felt the hard stares of his accomplices. He could feel support for his cause waning. Even *he* had learned in this country that was foreign to him that American men had respect for the women who had followed them into the danger of the West. Manfred needed to get them back in his fold.

Looking around to the changing faces and hearing the shuffling feet he made an announcement.

"Let's lighten the mood a bit, men," he said with a smile as he opened a cabinet against the wall, which revealed racks of whiskey in labeled bottles which not many of them had seen often. "This is the best whiskey Europe produces. And for tonight," he hesitated as he looked around the room, "it's all yours."

Ben Franks nodded his agreement to Manfred's tactic. While Ben was the rational side of the kidnapping, he knew that this German was wise about men and money. He had learned to appreciate Manfred's evil side. The man knew how to trigger the temptation in the weak, the malice in the toughs, and the brutality in the seemingly gentle.

While Ben Franks was not a desperate man by nature, he had always had a hot side to him. It was Manfred who had bought him out of just such a predicament on a murderous night in Abilene. This ordeal was to be the debt repaid. While Franks didn't like the deal, he was at heart a loyal man. In his mind the integrity he showed was for the man who saved him from the noose, and not the woman who had showed her scarred face. That was someone else's business. Not his. Drunken men would not be a danger to their cause, he knew, because the woman was still inside the lodge with a dozen armed men. Making the men docile with booze would probably serve their ultimate purpose anyway, he thought. Dependent men are obedient men, he had learned.

Marilyn was visibly appalled at the lost interest from the men in the room. It only confirmed her lack of faith in most men. They were still weak because they favored the escape from their little lives that liquor brought over the high road of honor and righteousness. But, she thought, who was she to change eons of human nature? She was just a woman in a savage new land. She chose that life and her scar was proof enough that she knew that, and it was proof enough that she could survive the hard life as good as anyone else; man, woman or savage.

After an hour of drinking, Marilyn began to worry. The drunken men were slobbering, arguing, and challenging each other. Their irrational boldness from liquor was starting to permeate the heavy, now smelly air dirtied by burping and flatulating ogres. Some of them were looking her way. She covered herself under the buffalo hides in hopes they would forget she was there. She felt her scar but did not feel sorry for herself. While her revelation did not ultimately shock the gang in the room, she knew it may come in handy to her advantage. She tightened the hides around her and dozed off hoping she would be forgotten to the revelers.

THROUGH THE CLOUDED AND lightly snowing sky the sun tried in vain to poke some rays through the dense moisture that hung over the mountains. It couldn't. All it managed to do was dimly lighten the clouds to grey, just giving enough announcement that morning had arrived.

Winston Winchester Colt was talking to Big Thunder, whose nose was dripping. Winston hung the feed bag of oats over his pal's ears. Thunder was content; for the moment. His eyes blazed open, his ears peaked, and he raised his head to see who else was nearing him. It was Rocky.

"I think I can get inside," Rocky said to Winston.

"What? How?" Winston asked.

"The lodge has an outhouse attached. It hangs over the cliff to dump the crap and stuff down the canyon. I can crawl up the hole and get inside," Rocky winced at the realization of what he would encounter with such an invasion.

"That would be a disgusting encounter," Winston acknowledged to the man's expression. "Tell me more."

"I can walk on the cliff laterally and go up the hole. I'll need a shotgun, a rifle and a couple of pistols. They'll be surprised and I'll probably be able to get at a bunch of 'em before they can return fire. When you hear the noise, you all can make your way up and help me."

Winston thought for a moment, then offered, "There must be at least twenty of them still inside. How about we let old Cogsdell up there on the ledge pick a couple of them off first? That will bring most of the others to the front of the cabin which will give you time to get a lot of them inside. When the shooting starts inside, me and the others will charge the lodge and try to get inside to help you." Winston hesitated and thought for a moment. He stroked Thunder's neck. "Are you sure about this? Chances are you're gonna be hit."

Rocky Mountain stood up straight and proud, smiled, and replied, "I'd gladly die for Marilyn Montgomery if God calls on me to make that sacrifice. I'm going to wrap my chest and neck with elk hide strips to maybe stop some of the bullets. Hell, sir, but if I die…I don't mind for this cause." Rocky felt the emotion which was dulling his fear.

"In my mind, a friend is someone who would sell everything they own to save someone else's life. You just pledged everything. No one is a better friend than you," Winston choked, putting his other hand on Rocky's now tearing cheek.

"It's time for us to be men," Rocky ordered, turning away to ready himself for his ultimate offering.

Big Thunder was finished eating and impatient. He had felt the electricity of testosterone before and he was ready and eager to join in the coming fray. Winston smiled at his prancing in place horse.

"Yeah, big guy, you're gonna be a part of this, too," Winston assured.

ROCKY WAS WRAPPED IN LEATHER strips and covered in a thick bear skin coat. Winston walked over and drove his fist as hard as he could into the man's stomach. Rocky did not flinch.

"Thanks for the test," Rocky laughed. "I'm not going to try to talk you out of this, Rocky, but what's the real reason you're doing this?" Winston sincerely inquired.

Rocky smiled a big, broad Cheshire cat grin. He looked straight into Winston Colt's eyes.

"I'm going to tell you only because I may never see you, or anybody, ever again. I have just one condition, however."

"Whatever you want."

"If I die, I want you to tell my son, Abraham, everything I'm about to tell you. If I live, you will never tell anyone."

"Deal."

"Abraham never knew his mother. My wife, Ambrosia, died giving birth to our son at the Double M Ranch. Winston, Ambrosia was the tenderest person I've ever known. She had a glow about her like an angel. Her skin was as dark as night with no stars. She looked like our ancestors must have looked in Africa. Her nose was flared like a powerful lion, her hair curled in rows like corn silk, and she walked softly like she was always on a cloud. She was a magnificent creature. I am still proud to know her."

Rocky Mountain was a big masculine man that others were proud to know, but he was weeping.

"She was proud," he continued, "from a tribe called Zulu. Tall. Slender. Perfectly formed in every way. She had a nobility that any queen would beg to have. And she chose me to bear her son. That's what I will carry with me to my end. But, I will tell you one other thing…Marilyn Montgomery stood by us with everything she had. She loved my wife. She loves me. She loves Abraham. No person ever said anything against me or my son when she did not stand up and offer all that she had to defend us. Marilyn Montgomery is my friend, yes. And I would rather die than betray that friendship. I will save her."

There was more than a moment of silence. Even Thunder somehow knew not to whinny or snort.

"I would not know what to offer in response," Winston whispered, trying not to tear.

"Well," Rocky continued, "Buck Krupp is convinced that Marilyn is Abraham's mother."

"What?" Winston popped, surprised.

"That's right. No one ever saw my wife when we came here. I visited the MM looking for work. I sent for Ambrosia four months after I'd been

91

established in the job. She came by wagon train. Abraham was born two months after that. I saw Krupp courting Marilyn in his forceful ways. I never interfered out of respect for Miss Marilyn, but I knew she did not like him. I would be there in the shadows. When he crossed the lines of a gentleman, I would step into the light. He said things. Bad things. Nasty things. He knew nothing of Ambrosia. She was fifty feet away in our cabin, but he didn't know she was lying in a bed sick and with child. Mr. Colt, the things he said about me and Marilyn sickened me. But, the lady she is, the lady my wife was, they would not let me interfere. Buck Krupp is sure that Abraham is a bastard and I aim to prove him wrong and end this evil plan he and his brother have hatched to profit from something that is a lie. It may kill me, but I will surely take them with me. If this is when I am to meet my Ambrosia, then so be it."

"I...I am at a loss," 'Winston said. "Men like you are surely a blessing in this unforgiving world."

"Then let's get on with it," Rocky declared, "let's lead them to the gates of hell."

With no other words the two men grasped each other with full hand and wrist in the gladiators' grip. Their eyes locked and their souls steeled. They were going to war.

THE SUN WAS ABLE TO OCCASIONALLY get a long ray through the mist that could sweep over the porch of the lodge. Harry Cogsdell watched each interval of light as it lit up a man walking the walkway surrounding the lodge. His Schutzen rifle was pointed in their direction. He looked to the sky and saw a small opening in the clouds promising a multiple ray. He thought that God must be on his side to allow him to kill devils today.

The first ray of light swept the porch allowing Harry to squeeze the hair trigger, releasing a large bullet to find its mark in the chest of a devil, which flew backwards from the impact. It was a five hundred foot shot. Then there was darkness under the eave covering the porch.

The second ray of light was ten seconds behind but it illuminated the porch instantly as though a dark lamp was lighted by the flare of a dry match. Three men who thought they could help their fallen comrade on the once dark porch were suddenly surprised and blinded by the change from dark to blinding light. Harry dropped the first man in the first split second of illumination. Never could he remember ejecting the bolt so quickly to reload, getting his eyes adjusted to the scope again, and hitting a target dead center again. He instinctively touched the trigger and the second man's head was split from his forehead to the back of his skull as the bullet ripped it in half. The ray of light swept past and then there was darkness again.

The third man dropped in fear over his fallen devil comrades. He lay in the darkness hoping he would not be seen. When the third ray of light suddenly illuminated the porch he stayed put. Seeing no movement, but while still aiming true, Harry withheld his next volley. The light dimmed to darkness again. The third man looked around, then bolted for the door of the lodge.

Harry saw something flash on the porch. He fired the Schutzen at it. The bullet hit the running man square in the waist where the silver concha adorned his belt. The lead entered his body and came out the other side taking off most of his private parts. As he stumbled through the door he wasn't dead; yet.

"Awwwwwww...." the third man wailed, "I bin' kilt."

There were twenty men before Harry Cogsdell started his war. Now there were only sixteen inside for Rocky Mountain to deal with.

"You were hired to deal with my security," Manfred Krupp yelled at Ben Franks.

"Damn that sharpshooter," Franks yelled back. "We've still got her to bargain with," he offered, nodding towards Marilyn.

With no one guarding the outside of the lodge, Winston Colt moved forward up the road with Thunder in tow. It was still very dark, which offered some cover. He motioned for two men to climb the sides of the hill to the cabin porch.

Winston knew that Rocky must be near the base of the backside of the hill where the crapper emptied out. He watched as the two other men made their way to the porch. He hoped for another ray of light so they could see who might next exit the lodge. But he saw no light and no movement.

The trail to the lodge was wet, dark and slippery. Winston knew that most horses would not venture on such a surface because of their doubting depth perception. However, Big Thunder was not most horses. He was about to trust the faith of his companion.

A very faint ray of light opened the cloudy sky enough to see that the two men had made it to the bottom of the porch. They waved at Winston that they were in position. Winston was atop Thunder, listening for the first shot promised by Rocky.

Rocky had just made it to the bottom of the crapper which was about six feet square and made of wood. He saw some human waste slop against the rocks before sliding off into the yonder of space to the canyon floor below. Piss was blowing around in circles into the air then it floated like rain caught by the eternal winds creating a stinking yellow whirlwind. He was glad he brought the rain slicker, too, which he promptly used to cover his buffalo coat and head. This was not going to be a pleasant climb, he thought.

He had slung his Henry so that he could raise the gun up from his hip. He checked that both of the Colts in the cross draw buscadero holsters were fully loaded. If he surprised the band in the lodge, he felt he could get ten of them before being hit himself. If he was agile and sly, he may get 'em all. However, he hoped that Winston and the others could get inside in time to kill their share. Loaded and ready, Rocky Mountain looked out over the great divide to the peaks that were his namesake. He took one last inhale of clean mountain air and then he pulled his kerchief over his mouth and nose, then he climbed down on the rock ledge that allowed him to enter the chute of the latrine.

It was dark in that cavern. And the smell was nearly intolerable, but luckily deadened by the cold and wet that cleaned the rocks. Rocky was thinking that if not for the quest to save Marilyn, he would have doubts. But, there was no longer any time to think. Now was the time to get done the things of men.

Rocky used the little light available at the bottom of the chute to climb the first ten feet of the fifty rocks he would have to scale. When it was too dark to see the rock crags where he could grip, he waited hoping that a ray of light would shine between the cracks in the wood slats to allow some vision. He could feel that the crap and piss was caking on his gloves. Then the sun broke the clouds. A stroke of luck for him, he thought, but not for his comrades on the other side of the lodge. He looked and saw that the lantern's light was faintly coming from the hole of the toilet's seat. No one was sitting on it at least. Then he saw the ladder of wood two-by's nailed to the back wall of the chute. He was relieved that the rest of the trip would be easier. He stepped onto the first rung and made his way upwards.

Winston saw what appeared to be the glint of light from a rifle barrel coming from the lodge. He was mounted on Thunder so he backed him away to behind a large pine. The two men under the porch stayed glued against it so they couldn't be seen. However, Harry Cogsdell saw the glint of light as well; and he did not miss the opportunity. Harry placed one shot directly into the breach of the rifle that protruded from the side of the lodge. The now useless weapon dropped to the porch. No one dared exit the door of the building to retrieve it.

While this distraction occurred, Rocky had been able to climb to just beneath the toilet seat. He was thankful that he saw no flesh darken the hole. He poked his head up into the small toilet room. He heard no noise. He also realized that his shoulders would not fit through the hole without taking off his heavy coat. The crud on his raincoat and gloves was sickening, but he quickly braced himself on the ledge and striped them off. He squeezed himself up the seat hole, hooked the door latch inside, and then looked through a slit in the door.

Men were looking out the windows on the other side of the lodge. He saw Marilyn in her corner. He saw Manfred Krupp and Ben Franks arguing in the opposite corner. Others were sitting, but most were standing and checking their firearms. Rocky was planning who to take first. He chose the leaders.

There was darkness as the sun was blanketed by the dark clouds again. Then someone pulled on the latched crapper door. His opportunity to take out the nearest enemy presented itself. Rocky unhooked the door and stood to the dark side of the crapper. The intruder pulled hard again and opened the door and entered. Rocky swiftly pulled the man inside and slit his throat with a ten inch Bowie blade. He stuffed the man's head into the hole of the crapper, lifted his body vertically and let him plunge into the hole. Then Rocky entered the room.

No one seemed to notice him at first. He walked directly to the corner where Krupp and Franks were standing and fired two shots. Krupp dropped, but Ben drew instinctively and his bullet hit Rocky in mid body, turning him sideways and causing Ben's next shot to miss and whiz by Rocky, whose outstretched arm exhibited a well aimed pistol that sent a bullet between Ben Franks' eyes. The elk hide had saved Rocky's life.

Marilyn sat up instantly and stared wide eyed at her friend. She took advantage of the surprise and grabbed a kettle of hot coffee and threw the liquid into the face of the outlaw nearest her. It was Bear Henry. When he reached for his pained face, she grabbed for the Smith & Wesson break top .44 stuck in his belt. It was heavy, she thought. She pulled the hammer back and blasted the man in the midsection. He fell over backwards as the huge bullet cut his spine in half.

With the first shot, Big Thunder was spurred to a gallop towards the muddy road up to the lodge. The two men waiting at the porch jumped up and let loose two double shotgun barrels into the front door, blowing it to pieces. The distraction allowed Rocky to empty his Henry into five more outlaws. Seven down and nine to go.

Everyone in the room had weapons drawn and were firing either at the doorway or at Rocky. The two men who had blasted the door were now firing their pistols through the open door, causing many men to back away. And then louder than an army of gunfire came a deafening cacophony of heaven's rolling thunder that resounded throughout the valley and shook the lodge as though an earthquake had hit it. It seemed like the lodge was moving on its own, which disoriented the men inside.

Winston atop his equine Thunder blasted through the door with guns ablaze. The shock of the weather and view of three Colts and a stallion startled a few of the men. Thunder raised up and crashed his front hooves across the shoulders of one of the outlaws. When Thunder came down he turned then jumped to a capriolet jutting his front and back legs outward to hit two more of his enemies who flew across the room like crumpled dolls. Snorting and prancing, he looked around for who was to be next.

A bullet grazed Winston's cheek. Instantly both gleaming Colt's pointed at the threat and in a simultaneous blaze two bullets ripped the man's heart in half. He fell in front of Rocky who expended the last bullets in his own pistols. Then there was dead silence. Everyone, except the rescuers was on the ground in some form of distress.

Rocky was finally able to make his way to Marilyn who gratefully hugged him. The two men who had blasted the door checked the dead and injured. The wounded were quickly conceding. Ben Franks was dead from the bullet between his eyes.

Micah Curtis and Buck Krupp walked into the room.

"Good timing," Winston quipped.

Micah smiled. He looked around the room and jammed his pistol barrel into the side of Buck and shoved him over to where Manfred was lying. Buck knelt down over his brother. Manfred moaned.

"Nice family," Winston said sarcastically.

"The worst," Micah agreed. "Got a posse comin' with wagons to clean up this mess. What say we mosey on outta here and back to civilization?

"Well, there's coffee on the stove over there. How about I buy ya a cup first," Winston answered, dismounting. When he did he saw Thunder's tail raise up. Winston turned the horse's rear towards the Krupps. A blast of wet digested hay and oats hit the two men like cannon shot. "Sorry, guys," Winston feigned, "guess ol' Thunder here had a bit too much water with his feed today."

Micah chuckled. Rocky howled in laughter. Marilyn smiled and nodded approval.

"Eee-yew, that's way too good for those guys," Abraham yelled from the door, then he looked around the room and ran to his father and threw his arms around him.

CHAPTER TWELVE

THE SHOOTERS AND THE SHOOTISTS

The contestants lined up to sign in. The whole town was still abuzz with the events of the week before and so much so that every night had been like Saturday after roundup. Also, the rumors of the gunmen that took part in the rescue had already circulated throughout the entire territory. Winston looked around. He didn't particularly like what he saw. There looked to be a few reputation seekers; a breed he loathed.

There were several categories being set up to measure the shooting prowess of each gunman. Winston had suggested that there be professional and amateur classes of shooters. Some, like himself he explained, shot guns for a living while others shot only when they needed to. At the end the amateur winners could take on the professionals. All tolled there were fifteen professional "shootists" as they were called and fifty non professionals. Micah was in charge.

"Your name," he asked without looking at the person standing before him.

"Duke, J.T.," came the deep drawling voice.

Micah slowly raised his head. He looked the man straight in the eyes. Duke smiled.

"Been a while, J.T.," Micah said.

"It has, Micah," Duke replied. "Prob'ly since we rounded up the Horseshack gang; 'bout five years, I reckon."

"Suppose so. You still freelancin'?"

"Pays better than Marshal'n. No offense, old friend."

"None taken. Glad to see you. You'll be shooting against Winston Colt. Family owns the maker."

"I know who he is. Has a reputation as a decent fella."

"There's some others here I could normally have arrested if they'd walked into town. You'll be shootin' against them, too," Micah warned.

"Any bounties available?" Duke asked, raising his eyebrows. "I mean, for after the competition, of course."

"Probably not if you lose," Micah grinned. "See ya in a bit...old friend."

"Jedidiah Johnson reporting, Mr. Curtis," came the first young voice.

"Dude Magee, Marshal, sir," proudly spoke the next young voice.

The people around the table laughed in unison. The boys turned their heads and frowned from the lack of respect.

"We can shoot as good as most men can," Dude announced.

"I know you can boys, but we don't have a kids category," Micah apologized.

A man yelled from the crowd, "Make a place for 'em Micah. They might just be marshals in training," he joked, as the crowd laughed then applauded the idea.

Micah couldn't stop a broad smile from sweeping his face, then he decided, "Then that's how it'll be. We have a category for under sixteen years of age, as that's when boys turn to men around here. I've seen both of you boys go to school then work for your folks. You could be men now anyway in my book. Sign up then, and pay the entrance fee."

"Entrance fee?" the boys gulped in unison.

"I got'em covered," Winston announced, as he dropped two brand new twenty dollar gold pieces on the table. "Never know, Marshal, they may be workin' for me someday instead of you. I consider it an investment."

The crowd applauded again.

"Okay, let's get everyone signed up so we can get on with this affair," Micah spoke more officiously.

Winston's eye was caught by Marilyn Montgomery riding into town atop a beautiful, large black and white paint mare that had a forehead blaze that looked like the letter M and a long black mane that dropped almost to her stirrups. She rode straight and proud upright in the saddle, which was covered in gleaming sterling silver tooled works of art. She rode over to where the people were signing up for the competition. She dismounted and tied the horse to a rail, turned, then looked directly at Winston. He hadn't seen her since they delivered her to her ranch the week before. Winston took in the whole vision of a magnificent figure of this courageous and brave woman.

Marilyn wore her trademark black pleated skirt that tickled the top of the black boots with the red MM cutouts that matched her blood red blouse and hair under a black flat brimmed hat. There were two things different about her this time, Winston noticed. The first was that she was wearing a silver concha adorned black left handed holster with polished .44 caliber bullets encircling the belt. And the other was that her hair was pulled back in a long pony tail. She was smiling; proud and unashamed. She made no attempt to hide the dark craggy scar that made an uneven line from the corner of her mouth to her right ear. Marilyn Montgomery walked right up to the sign up table and dropped her twenty dollar gold piece in front of Marshal Micah Curtis.

"I'll shoot with the other amateurs and hope I win so I can see how well you big bad gunmen do against this little ranch lady," Marilyn said in a very sexy southern drawl.

"I guess you intend to be the distraction to us professionals," Winston chimed in.

"I'm the weaker sex. I have to take every advantage I can," she answered looking directly into his eyes.

"You? Weaker? Ha!" he answered, then looked at the crowd, "Does anyone believe that?"

"Noooooooooooo!!!" came the chant from the crowd.

"There ya have it, young lady, we all know a ringer when we see one. We look forward to the competition, ma'am," Winston finished, sweeping his hat across his body as he bowed respectfully like the gentleman he liked to think he was.

She curtsied, then signed her name.

"How about dinner later?" Winston whispered.

"Sure," she winked.

"Anybody else?" Micah hollered to the crowd. "Anyone else to sign up?"

Buck Krupp pushed his way gently through the crowd. He had a box under his arm.

"Micah," Buck offered, "I want to donate this custom boxed set of pistols to the winner. I'm embarrassed about what my brother did. He deserves what he's gonna get."

"That's mighty generous, Buck," Micah agreed.

Then Buck turned to the crowd and announced loudly, "The Krupp family offers it's apology for the events of the past week. To show our good hearts, we are giving as a prize this custom set of pistols to the winner of the professional division of pistol shooters. Besides that," he paused, waved to his servant, Reinhardt who came forward arms loaded, "we are offering these other weapons to the winners of the various divisions. I hope this makes up for some of the disgrace caused by my family. Good luck to everyone."

The contestants gathered to look at the weapons, then dispersed; very impressed by the array.

Micah stood up from the table, closed the books, then announced, "First prize to the professionals in each class is $250. Overall best gets a $250 bonus. Amateur classes get $100 each, but overall best also gets a $250 bonus. Judges are me, Paddy McIrish, and Harry Cogsdell. Registration closed."

"That ain't fair," came a voice from the crowd. "I come here directly to shoot against Cogsdell."

"Who's that?" Micah asked.

"Horatio Wilfred Magillicuddy," came the reply. "I'm the best long distance hunter west of the Ozarks and I aim to prove it."

"Well, Billy," Harry started, "I know you to be one of the best around, but I'm needed to be a judge, so I stepped down from this competition for that reason."

"Sorry, sir," came another voice, soft and respectful, from near the table, "but, I think I can outshoot you, Mr. Cogsdell. My pa weaned me on long rifles and I can shoot the eye outta a ram on a rock at a thousand yards."

"Abraham," Rocky Mountain chastised, "that's not…"

"Pa, I'm bein' respectful like you taught me. I saw Mr. Cogsdell shoot and I know he's good. But, with his rifle, that fancy one with the eye scope, I bet I could have done the same as him. That's why I'm shooting in the professional competition."

"Against me, too, son," Buck asked with raised eyebrows.

"No sir, I'm shooting long distance single shot, not lever action carbine like you," Abraham corrected.

Micah piped up, "Sorry, gentlemen, but there's to be no long distance shooting because the competition is here in town. We've decided to limit it to modern weapons this time."

"How about this," Cogsdell offered, "I'll shoot a demonstration round with the three best of the lever action shooting competition. I took this job as a favor to Micah, not because I think I can outshoot everyone. Heck, this young man could be right about his marksmanship. We'll just settle the matter later."

"Sounds fair ta me," Billy agreed.

"Guess I'm shooting against you after all, pa," Abraham whispered.

Rocky nodded and smiled.

"AMATEURS ON THE NORTH MAIN STREET course and professionals on the south," Micah yelled.

There were about twenty professionals that strolled to the South course and at least fifty amateurs to the North.

People had set up chairs on the boarded walks, on the roofs and in the shops. They could turn their heads and watch the results of both competitions. Hay bales had been stacked up to ten feet tall and along the sides so as to stop the targeted bullets and hopefully any strays. No one was allowed in front of the firing lines. The first to start was the quick draw shooting for the amateurs.

At the other venue, the professionals started with lever action rifles. Since the real cowboys and lawmen depended most on longer range than pistols, the experience of the competition was fierce. Rocky Mountain and a man from Montana cattle country were dead even. Neither could miss a target. They were set for a final shoot off a bit later.

There were only a handful of under sixteen year old pistol shooters that could draw fast and accurate. Dude Magee and Jedidiah Johnson stood proudly together as even in the competition. Since they were better than anyone had thought, they were allowed to advance to the amateur men's group. No one complained after seeing their prowess with the weapons.

When the smoke cleared, there were four who made the final cut. Dude Magee, with his red hair wiring from under his black bowler hat missed on a shot at walking the can down the street; so made it only to fifth place, and thus was eliminated. He patted Jedidiah on the back and shook his hand.

"It's those long fingers of yours," Dude said to his friend, "they're gonna win it for ya."

"Thanks, Dude, ya done real good," Jedidiah complimented.

Winston Colt, standing in back of Jedidiah, tapped him on the shoulder and whispered, "Slow down now, and don't think. Just do what you've been doin' and let your eyes tell the bullets where to go. What you see is what you will hit. Don't' waiver. I see you copied my rig some."

He winked at the boy, now a man, and Jedidiah smiled in appreciation as he took a relaxing deep breath.

"We're gonna do it a bit different now," Micah announced. "We have this spring contraption that throws two tin cans at the same time. Each of you will have a can go over your head and out in front of you. The one who puts the most holes in the can wins."

The first two men stood side by side. The cans appeared over their heads. One gunman pulled his first shot off into the ground. Before the can hit the ground he was able to get off two more shots. Only one hit the can. His opponent tried fanning his gun and missed altogether. That left it for Jedidiah and the young cowboy to face the flying cans. They looked at each other and smiled. They were taking it in the spirit of a sporting competition, not a gunfight.

Jedidiah lifted the pistol from his holster. He had modified the rig a bit after seeing Winston's holster the week before. It fit the cylinder better because he had whetted the leather to stretch to shape, thus making it slide easy in and out. He also wore the belt a bit lower so his long forefinger pointed right at the trigger guard when his arm hung relaxed at his side. He checked to be sure all six bullets were in their nests. He was using lighter loads and lighter grain bullets to prevent recoil. He had learned that from gunsmith Paddy McIrish.

Jedidiah had done extra work for Paddy so as to get lessons in shooting as well as the care and respect for firearms. Jedidiah's parents had been lost in a snowstorm trying to cross the mighty Rockies in a false spring. The wagon train had been cut in half by an avalanche while his folks were in the lead wagon and Jedidiah, an infant, was in the last wagon with the other babes who were being kept extra warm. The survivors made it back to Sage Brush where Jedidiah was given to the care of a storekeeper's family. He grew up earning his keep and learning to respect and appreciate kindness. But he had a mean streak that his caretakers hoped he had learned to control. With the mentoring of Paddy as well, Jedidiah seemed even tempered and amiable; until something would set off his explosive temper. There was no reason for his temper to flare this day; or so he thought. However, while his cowboy competition was dressed in normal working clothes including leather chaps, Jedidiah was dressed in all black, including his hat. He looked slick and ready. Winston noted the attention to detail in the young man's clothing and wondered about his developing self image. He hoped it wasn't a vision as a gunfighter.

Jedidiah's left handed gun and the competitor's right hand rig were on the outside of the pair standing in the street. They were both set and ready.

The cans whistled over their heads. The cowboy drew his 7 ½ barreled Colt very smoothly so as to be sure to clear the holster. The first shot popped the can up another ten feet, giving him more time to hit it again…and hopefully again.

Jedidiah's 4 ¾ inch barrled Colt had cleared the holster faster and his first shot also hit his can dead on, but pushed the can not only up but further away. He did not think about that. His young eyes were focused on the can. His right hand crossed over and he fanned the hammer five more times. If three seconds had passed that would have surprised everyone. It was over very quickly.

The cowboy had cocked his hammer after each shot and was able to get off only four total before the tin can hit the dirt. Judge Paddy McIrish jogged his thick, muscled body down the street and picked up the cans.

"The cowboy's can," Paddy yelled, "six holes. Jedidiah's can, six holes." He then turned the can to look at the top and then corrected, "Check that...there's eight holes. Jedidiah wins!"

The citizens in the crowd who knew Jedidiah cheered, while Jedidiah instinctively twirled the gun back into its holster. Winston noted the ease and comfort the boy handled the weapon without thinking or feeling for the holster. It reminded Winston of himself as a boy obsessed with guns. He knew he would have to spend some time with Jedidiah to help set his talent in the right direction. Winston's dark, cold side crept into his brain. He had learned to control his temper, but he was beginning to remember some of his own history. He took a deep breath and tried to rid his mind of that for the time being.

Winston heard more gunshots and then the announcements for the winners. The winner of the women's rifle contest was, by no surprise, Marilyn Montgomery. The professional lever action rifle competition was just ending, so he walked over to see what was happening.

Micah held his hand up. "It's a tie so far," he announced. Rocky and Abraham Mountain and Horace McGillacuddy are tied. Set up the bottles 50 yards further away," he yelled.

George guided his wagon to the wooden shelves that were 150 yards away now. He set up six bottles for each shooter onto the four parallel shelves so that the vessels were in a circular pattern which would cause the shooters to have to rotate their barrels and change elevation with each shot. With eighteen bottles set, George got out of the line of fire.

"Here's the deal for this round," Micah instructed, "When I say go, you will all shoot at the same time. You can shoot the bottles in any order, but you only have ten seconds. So, shooters ready?"

Rocky held his big old brass octagonal barreled Henry at his side ready for the order to fire six big old .44 rimfire bullets at their marks. It was the same gun he used when Winston saw him win years before. Abraham used a Winchester Model 73 in lighter loaded .32-20 caliber. Horace rested on his shoulder the barrel of an older and well used Winchester Model 1866 Carbine also in .44 caliber. They stood about six feet apart and when Micah spoke, they all brought their weapons to their shoulders.

Micah began his chant, "Ready…set………go!"

The noise was deafening and the smoke was blinding. The Henry used old black powder ammo that smelled like war. Looking down the range everyone could see glass splattering in all directions. Rocky patterned his motion clockwise starting from the high noon position. It wasn't more than 7 seconds when Rocky stopped firing. He looked down the range certain he had blasted to bits all of the bottles. He glanced at the middle targets that Abraham was shooting at. Two seconds later both Abraham and Horace stopped firing, their ammo spent.

George emerged to check the targets. He turned with a megaphone in his hand and yelled, "Rocky, six. Abraham and Horace, five each."

Horace threw his rifle to the ground. Abraham, happy that he had been good enough to even compete with his father turned and smiled pridefully at him.

"I'm awfully proud to be second to you, Pa," the boy stated.

"You aren't second place yet, son," Rocky said, "It looks like you'll have a shoot off for that privilege."

Abraham turned his head to only meet Horace's glaring eyes drilling into his own. Abraham gulped.

"You men wanna see who's second?" Micah asked.

"Darn tootin', Marshal," Horace spat, while Abraham shrugged his shoulders and nodded agreement.

"Okay, then, how's about you load up eight shots each and see who gets the most? We'll give you twelve seconds this time. Agreed?"

Both men nodded while quickly reloading and checking their weapons.

Rocky leaned over to Abraham's ear and whispered, "You're breathing too hard. It's only a contest. Take some deep breaths and relax. You've already won in my book."

Abraham smiled, took a few breaths and then raised his rifle to his shoulder.

"Ready…set…go!" Micah yelled.

Looking down range the crowd saw glass flying in all directions. When the smoke cleared George again ran downrange to check the results and yelled, "Horace, six bottles. Abraham, seven bottles."

Abraham turned towards Horace and held his arm out to shake Horace's hand. He could not look the defeated adult directly in the eyes so he hung his head.

"Young man," Horace spoke firmly, "hold yer head up and look at me square in the eyes like the man you are." When Abraham obeyed Horace firmly took the lad's hand in a man's handshake and continued, "That was mighty fine shootin'. You beat me fair and square. I'd be proud to hunt with you anytime." Then he smiled broadly.

"Why, thank you, sir," Abraham said, "guess I was pretty lucky."

"T'weren't luck, young man. And don't call me sir again. You shoot like a man so's act like a man. You call me Horace here on out. I'm proud to know ya. You an' yer pa come see us. My wife makes the best biscuits in the West."

Rocky placed his hand on Abraham's shoulder and nodded a thankful approval to Horace for his kind words.

"Final events comin' up, so everyone listen up," Micah shouted ending the celebrations of the riflemen. "Professional pistol shooters gather round. We have two contests. The first is for accuracy. The second is for accuracy with speed. You can change your weapons for each of the contests if it's to your liking. Load up and get set."

Winston was standing at ease at the firing line ready for the first contest. He assessed his competition. He thought it curious that Buck Krupp would compete, but in fact he was innocent of any complicity in the kidnapping matter. He carried two blued Colt Navy's in cross draw holsters at his side. They looked to be in .44 caliber and engraved. Another man could have been Wild Bill Hickock's ghost come back to show off his skills still dressed in a tassled jacket and long curly blond hair straggling past his handle bar mustache, except that he had two nickel plated Colt Army's in obvious .45 caliber of 5 ½ barrel length for modest accuracy at longer distances but still quick out of the holster. Then there was a working cowhand who curiously wore a Smith & Wesson .44 Russian in a shoulder holster. It looked to be an earlier single action.

And finally he saw a man decked out all in black. The necks of his shiny black boots were tall over his pants legs. His custom holster rig had a sterling silver heart on each holster and was slung low below his waist and tied to his legs just above the knees. It held two 4 ¾ inch barrel Colt's, probably in .45 caliber he thought, with a long horn steer head in raised relief carved on the aged, yellowed ivory grips. The man's eyes could not be seen due to his flat brimmed hat tilted down nearly to the man's eyebrows and casting a dark shadow across his face. He did make out something peculiar though. It appeared that the man was wearing dark eyeglasses that had small round lenses, which he has seen before but only worn by long distance shooters. The man appeared to be staring directly at Winston. And he did not move to the shooting line.

The overly dramatic mystery man tipped his hat at Winston and his clean shaven face broke open to gleaming white teeth when the man smiled. Winston winked at the man, who then stopped smiling. He hung his thumbs on the silver buckle holding the gun belt. Winston felt the glare from the man's unseen eyes.

"Were gonna make this interesting," Micah announced. "We're gonna again use this here contraption with a spring or somethin' in it that will throw two cans this time in the air at equal time, speed and distance. Each of you gets to shoot at the two cans with your pistols already drawn if you choose. We'll see who gets eliminated and then go to the final.

The cowhand successfully fired a shot from his Russian into each of the cans, as did Buck Krupp. When his turn came, Wild Bill drew both guns and also hit both cans.

Winston wore a set of blued Colt .45's with 7 ½ inch barrels housed in a tooled brown leather rig with a Colt horse embossed on the silver buckle. He calmly drew only one of the pistols and easily blew holes in both cans.

"Now we've got a competition here," Micah cheered as the crowd yelled in agreement. "So, now we'll put four cans in the air and see how you all do."

The cowhand looked nervous but he stood at the ready, but almost like he was about to embark on a footrace. The cans flew in the air. His gun had been drawn but he was able to only get off three shots, hitting two cans. He shook his head and stepped back.

Buck Krupp had a pistol in each hand. When the cans flew he hit two right away. He cocked the hammers back but did not pull the hammer on the left pistol to lock position. His right bullet hit another can leaving the fourth can to fall uninjured to the ground. He also stepped away.

Wild Bill drew his guns fast then twirled them back into their holsters. He cracked his knuckles and shook his body. "I'm ready, chief," he said. As the cans rose he hit two on the way up, recocked perfectly then hit the other two on the way down. He twirled the Navy's back home. "Now, that's what I'm talking about," he bragged.

J.T. Duke missed one can, so was eliminated, but he commented, "I was always better when them targets was shootin' back at me. Good luck gentlemen."

Winston strolled to the firing line. He pushed his large brimmed Paso hat back off his forehead then stood relaxed. "Hit it, Micah," he said with confidence.

He drew both pistols simultaneously and hit all four cans on the way up.

"Well, looks like we got another round to shoot," Micah affirmed. "Six cans, six bullets. You can use one pistol with six bullets or two pistols with three bullets each. Whatever suits you," he informed.

Wild Bill loaded three bullets into each of his two Navys. Winston loaded his left Colt only.

The cans flew in a pattern of three left and three to the right. Wild Bill drew both pistols and started firing and recocking. Through the smoke and noise no one could be sure what he hit. Cans were being pushed all over the sky. When they hit the ground George announced that he had hit four cans. Wild Bill proudly spun his pistols back into their holsters and strutted before the crowd.

Winston Colt was a professional shootist. He remembered handling guns before he remembered using a fork to eat. He spun the cylinder of his left pistol to recheck for a full load. Then he executed a flat spin, an overhead spin, a forward draw, a reverse draw and then at least three twirls before the pistol slipped easily into its holster. Those who knew what he was doing noted the longer barrel length in awe that these moves were done with that long barreled pistol. He nodded he was ready.

The same pattern of cans that Wild Bill had, flew into the air. Winston easily drew the pistol and let go the first shot, then fanned it with his five fingers. All six cans flew in some different direction than they had started. George confirmed that all six had been hit. This part of the competition was over.

Marilyn walked over to Winston and said, "I don't think I'll try my luck after all. That's pretty good shooting, Mister."

"Yeah, *pretty* good?" Winston mocked.

She smiled and placed her forefinger on her lips then put it to his. Buck Krupp turned and walked away.

"Are all shootists ready for the speed competition?" Micah barked.

The man in black walked up to the line near where Winston was standing. His glasses darkened eyes were level with Winston's, who now saw that the man was lean, muscular and tight.

"Mighty fancy gunplay," he said to Winston.

"You're Texas Jack Blackman, right?" Winston asked.

"True."

"I've heard some things about you that I don't like."

"Such as?"

"You *like*... killing men."

"Only when they need killin'."

"That's not what I said. I said that you *like,* killing men."

"Hmm."

"Well, remember that this is only a competition. The only thing to kill around here holds beans."

"Really?" Jack mumbled, hesitated, then took a step back.

"*Really*," Winston emphasized.

Texas Jack turned away then looked over his shoulder and asked, "Hey, Mr. Colt…you eat beans?"

Winston wasn't amused and his fingers twitched instinctively near his pistols. Texas Jack backed away and held his hands up and laughed out loud.

"So, guess it's down to just the two of you gentlemen," Micah said, "the others have withdrawn. Here's what we'll do. That box with white lines on it up there about 25 paces in front of you has holes in the top. We're gonna put this hard boiled egg on top of the box. There's a trap door so that the egg will drop when we release the door. It will appear in that opening you see in the front of the box. As you can see, there are six openings in case we need that many. It's up to you to hit the egg as soon as you see it in the opening. The horizontal lines are six inches apart starting at a man's height from eye to waist level. We have two judges that will determine at which line the egg fell to when you hit it. You get one shot. This is a contest of speed *and* accuracy. As you know, a quick man may be a dead man, if you get my drift."

"You can say that again," a big woman in the audience jibed to laughter from the crowd as her elbow nudged a man who was probably her husband.

"Texas Jack," Micah directed, "you're first."

Jack walked up to the line. He cracked his knuckles and let his hands settle loosely to his side. He quickly drew both pistols in a reverse draw, cocked both hammers then let them lightly down and spun the pistols back. He drew again spinning the pistols twice then to a flat spin and then back again into the holsters. He looked over to Winston thinking he'd done a better exhibition with both guns. Winston smiled and shook his head.

"Ready anytime you are, Marshal," Jack declared.

The egg dropped. The crowd was silent.

The instant the first egg appeared Jack's pistol struck quicker than a desert hot rattler. He quickly spun the pistol back into its holster and stood up straight.

"Second line," Micah announced after talking to the two judges.

Texas Jack frowned.

Winston strolled to the firing line. He had changed rigs and guns. Strapped low on his hips was a smooth polished clean black twin leather holster rig with buckles around each holster, a solid silver belt buckle with the Colt trademark horse rearing in the center and polished *real silver* bullets encircling the belt. In it were two nickel plated, highly factory engraved, lightened and tuned Colt .45's with 5 $\frac{1}{2}$ inch barrels for better accuracy, and mother of pearl grips. He didn't need to spin them to show off this time. He was about to prove why he was the Colt factory representative.

When the first egg fell he quickly drew and hit the egg dead center, blasting egg pieces back into the box.

"Second line," Micah declared. "Okay, boys, we'll drop two eggs in the box and they'll come out of two different holes. You can use one or both guns. Same rules."

Using only his right pistol again, Jack hit both again on the second line. Winston shot the same.

"Well, this is remarkable. I've never seen anyone shoot as good as the two of you. Let's just drop six eggs this time and see who gets what!" Micah laughed.

"Six?" Jack questioned. "Can I use both guns?"

"Winston, what do you say?" Micah asked.

"If he needs two guns, he can use two guns," Winston replied.

"And you don't?" Jack challenged.

Winston smiled and shrugged.

"Set 'em up," Jack spat, "I'm ready."

When the six eggs appeared out of six separate holes, Texas Jack deftly unloaded at least eight shots before all of the targets were out of sight, one way or the other. He spun his smoking guns anxiously into their holsters.

"Five eggs hit," Micah announced.

Jack smiled, sure of victory.

Winston walked to the line and simply nodded his head.

The eggs dropped and Winston drew only his right pistol. The first shot hit the egg before it hit the first line. He had cocked the hammer for his first shot with his thumb, then followed by fanning each successive finger beginning with the index until the final shot with his little finger. He quickly and reactively spun the pistol home.

"Five eggs," Micah declared. "You two are very good, that's for sure. Any ideas how to settle this?"

"Yeah, I've got an idea," Texas Jack posed, "instead of eggs we use eyeballs. His and mine."

"Very funny, young man," Micah reacted taking it lightly.

"I think he means it," Winston responded, "but, you have two of those target boards. Set them up side by side. Drop twelve eggs in them and we'll see who hits the most of them."

"I can do that," Jack agreed, "but this time he goes first. And I need a break to get something cold to drink."

Winston smiled and nodded agreement. He began loading the right gun with shiny bullets as Texas Jack walked towards the saloon. Winston looked up suddenly just as Jack swung through the doors. Something didn't feel right to Winston. He went back to reloading his guns as someone set a glass of water in front of him. He looked up again.

"Are you parched, cowboy?" Marilyn asked.

"Yes and no," he replied as Marilyn raised her eyebrows. "Yes I'm thirsty but I'm no cowboy."

"Really?!" she wondered aloud.

"Cowboys work hard for a living. I grew up playing with big boy's toys."

She looked him up and down and parried, "Big boy working hard with his toys. Hmmm. Sounds interesting."

Winston's grin seemed to go past his cheeks and around his head. He was getting to like this woman. He dropped his pistol into its holster and gulped the water. He turned his head and saw Jack burst through the saloon's swinging doors and stroll quickly to the firing line. To Winston he seemed nervous. But no matter, there was tension in the air anyway.

"Get ready, gentlemen," Micah announced.

"Let the hens loose," Winston said standing relaxed and ready.

All of the eggs were loosed at once. Winston instantly decided he would try to take out as many eggs as possible on the right side first. He knew that he could get most by the time they hit the third line, but he knew that the left side's eggs would be at the third line before he got to them. He'd try to get as many of them as possible at that time.

He drew only the right Colt and executed his spread finger fan expending all six bullets then let it drop to the ground but had already drawn the left side and fanned it until empty. The crowd was awestruck. People knew this was not normal and obviously very lethal.

The results were screamed, "Six on the right, three on the left. Nine total."

To heavy clapping Winston holstered the left Colt then leaned down and picked up the right one he had dropped in the dust. He saw Jack's boots under his view. Winston raised and was eye to eye with his now nemesis. Jack smiled, but his lip twitched. Winston felt that same uneasiness again. He stepped back and let Jack square off on the line.

The twelve eggs dropped.

Jack drew both guns simultaneously and let loose with well timed and practiced volleys from both barrels. Winston instinctively counted the shots at eleven.

"Five on the right and four on the left," was the verdict.

The crowd was very audibly excited. Winston motioned his head at Marshal Micah Curtis to come over to where he was standing near the line.

"Nice shooting, Jack," Winston complimented. "I'm curious about the balance of your weapons. They seem to be very finely tuned. Mind if I hold one of 'em?"

Pumped with adrenaline Jack did not think to disagree or refuse. He handed Winston the left gun. Winston bounced it on his palm then slipped his finger through the trigger guard and spun, nodding in approval. He looked down the barrel and saw the tip of a bullet resting in its cylinder hole, confirming his count. By now a crowd was gathering around, including gunsmith and judge Paddy McIrish.

"Bullets are really important," Winston said matter-of-factly, "they make or break successfully hitting the target. Would you agree with that Paddy?"

"Aye, lad," Paddy agreed.

"Hey, you're the gunsmith," he added, tossing the pistol to Paddy, then added, "I'm interested in the gunpowder load and the grain of the lead, from a purely technical point of view. Take a look, will you?

Texas Jack Blackman was oblivious to the conversation and was in fact talking to a young female admirer. "Yeah, I got one more on the left side than old fancy pants over there did," he bragged, "he may work for the factory, but I'm the guy whose life depends on these guns." He touched both holsters then realized he was missing one of his weapons. He turned and joined the men looking over his Colt.

Paddy had the five spent and one loaded cartridges inside his closed fist. He held them out and dropped them into the hands of Micah. He spun the emptied pistol and handed it grip first to Texas Jack, who firmly took it.

"Huh!" Micah exclaimed, "There's one live bullet here."

Winston looked over at Jack, who seemed to be sweating.

Micah continued, "This bullet has been cut into four sections."

"That's a lie," Jack hollered, "let me see that. Hell, it's factory ammo."

"Nope," Paddy confirmed, "see right here, it's been quartered with two separate hemispherical cuts. Bullet acts like shotgun pellets. Man's a fraud, Micah."

Jack stepped back. He'd been found out. He caught the Marshal's disgusted stare and by that he suddenly knew that this was one lawman that didn't cotton to liars or cheats.

"Winner is Winston Colt," Micah announced to the crowd, then he turned to face the cheater. Texas Jack Blackman was not there. Micah noticed also that J.T. Duke, who had been standing beside Micah during the shoot off, was also gone.

Buck Krupp weaved his way through the crowd and stood before Winston. He held out the box containing the custom Colts that Winston himself had delivered.

"To the winner, sir," Buck offered, handing Winston the opened box displaying the guns.

Winston smiled and nodded as he looked into the crowd, then spotting what he was looking for and announced, "Would Jedidiah and Dude please both come up here!"

Arm in arm the boys, who Winston noted now stood tall like men, arrived in front of Winston.

"Boys, I'm proud of the way you handled yourselves here. These special custom Colts are a matched set and have consecutive serial numbers. The pistols are forever branded as blood brothers, just like I hope the two of you can stay for your lifetimes. I am hereby awarding you each one of these pistols. Now, the trigger guard can be replaced to fit your fingers, and I'm sure gunsmith Paddy can see to that, but the significance of this award is something I hope you never forget. This great nation was founded on each man's and woman's right to defend themselves. Our forefathers even wrote that down. You are entrusted with the right to own and keep firearms so that if ever there is a threat to our freedom that comes from without or within, you will already be armed to be a part of a militia that could not have hidden your weapons. That is our insurance as individuals against government. What that means, boys, is that you are *defenders,* not aggressors. You do not look for trouble, but you do not run from it either. We've all seen your proficiency with pistols. Now let us all hope that your friendship lasts and that you both follow paths of truth and justice." He looked at each boy and asked, "Which of you two is the older?"

Jedidiah held up his hand.

Winton held the guns upside down and checked the serial numbers then said, "Jedidiah, you get the earlier serial number," then he handed each boy his Colt and handed the case to Paddy McIrish. "And remember, this is a *matched set.* See that your hearts resemble that fact."

The audience clapped and cheered. The boys, awestruck, wandered off to admire their prizes.

"Okay, everyone, we'll have a thirty minute break. Winston and his horse will demonstrate some fancy shootin' on horseback with Winchesters and pistols. See ya back here then."

CHAPTER THIRTEEN
WHOA BIG THUNDER

Winston waited until Thunder had exhaled a second time then he pulled the sheepskin covered cinch as tight as it would squeeze against the horse's belly. He checked that the scabbard on the left side was set properly at the rear of the saddle with the butt of the twenty eight inch barrel Winchester Model 1876 within easy reach. He pulled the rifle and then loaded it with 5 rounds of .45-70 long range bullets. He had set up 4 large bottles at the far end of the street, so he had an extra round for insurance. He rubbed the octagonal barrel and saw the "One of One Hundred" in italic script at the base of the barrel reminding him that he had the only one of seven ever made that had a plain trigger. He did not lever a bullet into the chamber.

Winston walked around to the other side and checked that the right scabbard was set at a mirror position. He pulled the shorter twenty inch long round barrel Winchester Model 1873 out and held it. It was a fancy nickle and gold plated masterpiece with factory engraving and figures representing his horse, Big Thunder. He loaded the weapon with eight .44 WCF shells intended for six smaller bottles. He did not cock the lever, but rather screwed down a set pin drilled into the lever until it fully engaged the trigger. The lever was circular. He put the rifle back then walked to the front of Thunder and looped the rein over his neck and ducked under his chin to arrive at the mounting side of the horse. He then checked to reassure that he had properly reloaded his nickel plated Colts.

"Ready, boy?" he whispered in the horse's ear.

Big Thunder was beginning to prance and snort. He was well practiced in what was going to happen next. He had been born to a centuries old breed that was trained for battle with a warrior on his back. Riders did not need hands to communicate a command to an Andalusian horse. All of the commands were done by foot and leg. The rider was completely and confidently able to use both hands in battle without holding onto reins. However, to master this art took many years of training for both man and horse. When Winston mounted Big Thunder it was obvious that they had spent the time needed. Taking up the rein Winston collected him then easily guided Thunder to the starting line.

Bullhorn in hand, Paddy McIrish announced, "For your viewing and admiring pleasure, not to mention your... *jealous pleasure...*" he paused for his laugh, "Mister Winston Winchester Colt will demonstrate the fine art of shooting while astride his Andalusian stallion, Big Thunder. He will ride at full gallop to the end of the street first firing at four bottles with a Winchester '76 and then at four more with a Winchester '73. He will turn at the end of the street and then shoot four bottles on either side of him with his Colt .45's...at the same time. And all of this while moving! And all the time without reining the horse! That's *no hands* riding, friends!" The audience ooed and awed. "Ready, Mr. Colt?"

Winston gathered his rein so that Thunder's nose nearly touched his chest and then lightly spurred him, who understood the signal to levade up on his rear legs so that he was raised vertical to the ground while the rider waved his hat to the crowds' applause. When Thunder lowered to all fours he was snorting and ready to go.

The rein had a small hook that Winston attached to a ring on his belt buckle. He was now "hands-free." The distance on the rein kept Thunder's neck bent a bit for collection but still allowed him the freedom to move where and when he was instructed. Everyone could see that this was a fine tuned act that only a professional could ever perform. That was true, however, Winston had a credo on horseback. He had learned that to ride well is to be at one with the horse with only one brain thinking, so pay attention and don't let the horse think; you do and you may be dead. Winston was paying attention and Thunder was obeying every twitch of his other half's calf and touch of his spur.

Few had ever seen such horsemanship and appropriately the town fell dead quiet. Winston went into his mental serious mode. He spun Thunder three hundred sixty degrees then lightly touched his spurs alternately on Thunder's side causing the horse to prance in place in a piafe. He simultaneously squeezed his calves and the horse moved forward. Then he gave slight alternate tugs on each side of the rein while spurring lightly the opposite side of the horse causing him to thrust each leg alternately straight forward and parallel to the ground showing a Spanish Walk that was used to clear peasants from the path of royalty in medieval times. They were two hundred yards from the bottles at the end of the dirt street. Hands off the rein, Winston raised his legs up along Thunder's sides signaling him to stop, then he raised him into a levade then leaned forward causing the horse to drop to all fours at which time Winston applied a light spur to both sides of Thunder. The horse bolted.

In full on gallop and at one hundred seventy yards from the large bottles Winston reached down and pulled the Model '76 from it's scabbard and in one motion swung the rifle to his shoulder and stood up in the stirrups so the barrel of the weapon was at least a foot above Thunder's head and having levered the first shell into it's chamber pulled the trigger to blow apart the first bottle. The horse was moving so fast that the next three shots met their marks by the time the horse was now only one hundred yards from the last six smaller bottles. Winston holstered the Model '76 in its scabbard.

He then reached down on his right, pulled the Model '73 from its scabbard and held it to his side. He slowed Thunder to an easier trot then put him into a forty five degree side pass. When they were seventy five yards from the bottles he tossed the Winchester out in front of him as if to throw it. Caught by the loop lever, it cocked a round into the chamber. He pulled the rifle down to beside him at waist level. When the lever was set the screw in it hit the trigger to fire the first round and burst the first bottle to bits. Each successive of the next four lever actions caused a bottle to burst. Then he felt Thunder's body straighten. Winston had loosened the pressure on his left leg allowing the horse to think...cardinal rule broken. He missed the sixth bottle. Immediately making a correction, Thunder came back to form and he blasted the final bottle with one of his two remaining bullets. If the target had not been an inanimate object the result may have been different. He put the rifle back and turned his horse just in time to come within ten yards of the broken bottles. He headed back towards town.

He spurred Big Thunder into a full gallop again. Thunder was aimed dead center in the road and as he ran his back probably didn't gain or lose more than and inch of elevation. Winston noted that there were no people lining the street near a hundred feet on either side of the targets. Halfway down the street he drew both Colts and began shooting the bottles set up on opposite sides of the street. Both pistols fired simultaneously while his eyes were pointed straight ahead he relied on his peripheral vision...and years of rehearsal. Rating the speed of the horse with the course of the bullets was an unnaturally born art form, his family on both sides would often tell him, and, they added, his breeding for that form of art was impeccable. He hit all of the bottles, leaving him two rounds in each handgun.

When they reached the end of the targets he spun the guns into their holsters and legged Thunder to a sliding stop and yelled, *"Whoa, Big Thunder."*

The horse slid no less than thirty feet in a cloudy haze of dust in front of the applauding crowd. Then Winston saw something disturbing. A big black horse was stepping high towards them. The rider was all in black, had his split reins in his mouth and had his guns drawn. He spurred the black horse to a lope and then to a full on gallop. Winston did not relish anyone else trying these tricks and especially with innocent people possibly in the line of fire. Winston and Thunder stood their ground as if to warn the rider off. The first round from the rider's gun whizzed right by Winston's ear. It was now obvious that this gunman was not after inanimate targets. The crowd cowered against the store front walls and ducked for cover.

Winston was not going to charge the man and endanger Big Thunder. He spun the horse around, spurred him off down the road in the opposite direction and rolled off backwards flipping and landing on his butt in the dirt. He felt a bullet hit near his hand. As he turned he could now see that it was Texas Jack and not more than seventy five yards away.

He was blazing with both guns and his split bullets were throwing shot-like pieces of lead everywhere.

Winston stood up, hatless and filthy with road dirt but he had both Colts in his hands. However the dust in his eyes did not allow him to see clearly. Then he felt someone bump him to the side.

"Texas Jack Blackman, you're under arrest," yelled the man next to Winston, who through clouded eyes only saw the man's brown boots, who then ordered louder, "I'm takin' you dead or alive for murder."

The man's answer was a volley of shots from Texas Jack that rained a hail of lead in front of him with one piece of a quartered bullet tip that stung him in the leg.

"Jack, damn you," the man yelled. Then he raised his pistol and fired once.

With the first shot, although he was still blurry eyed, Winston knew what the weapon was. His defender had fired a behemoth of a pistol that let loose a devastatingly deadly .44 caliber oversized bullet that ripped bodies in half. The noise deadened Winston's left ear hearing for a moment and the wafting gunpowder poured into his nostrils. By the second shot the dirt had cleared from his eyes enough for him to see that the man who was shooting was J.T. Duke. The pistol, Winston confirmed, was a Texas Ranger issue nine inch barrel nearly five pound Walker Colt.

The first shot had hit Texas Jack in the left upper arm. The impact was so violent that it twisted his body ninety degrees as the arm was severed and flew off with his pistol still gripped in its now flying limb. Duke couldn't see that part, but the motion turned Jack's right hand so that the other Colt was pointed right at Duke and by reaction fired a shot at him. All J. T. saw was the aggressor now only twenty five yards away and blazing bullets at him and Winston. J. T.'s second shot hit Jack in the midsection. Duke thought for sure he saw daylight through the man.

Texas Jack fell limp in the saddle and back on his horse's withers. Horse and rider trotted between Duke and Winston until someone grabbed the fallen gunfighter's reins and stopped the horse. That was Marshal Micah Curtis.

"Well, Duke, I guess you have a warrant for Texas Jack?" Micah asked, raising an eyebrow.

"Well, old friend, I guess you musta knowed I wasn't here for no shootin' competition," the big man answered pulling a "Wanted Dead or Alive" poster from his vest pocket.

Micah threw his hands in the air and turned to the gathering crowd then announced, "Okay everybody, Texas Jack Blackman was a wanted man and this competition is formally over. So, you can all go celebrate at the town barbeque with beef sponsored by the cattleman's association, beans from the farmer's guild, and the beer and ades from the town bars and restaurants. Now git!!" he yelled, "And have a good time."

"Hey, thanks, John T.," Winston offered with hand outstretched.

Duke took it with his big bear sized paw and returned, "Nah, son, I gotta thank your family for makin' this here cannon. Hell, see how big the trigger guard is? Has ta be to fit these mitts. You alright?"

"Thanks to you, sir. I'm just a target shooter really. It's men like you that face off and rid this country of idiots like that one armed gutted body over there. No loss, that's for sure."

"Well, I'd say ya done yer fair share of makin' this country safe. Miss Montgomery told me what you did. I've known her since she was born. Knew her parents. She's a fine woman and I think of her as family. I'm kind of an...uncle, you might say. Get my drift?"

"No sir. What are you getting at?"

J.T. Duke gave Winston a mock surprise look and said, "I think she kind of likes you, young man. Just be a gentleman, that's all I ask. Just be a gentleman."

Winston smiled broadly, winked and nodded. No more words were needed.

EPILOGUE
WANDERING WITH TUMBLEWEEDS

inner with Marilyn Montgomery was delightful. Winston had never met such an intelligent and capable woman anywhere in his travels. She had the charm and poise of the most refined city lady but was spiced with real western savvy. How could he leave the perfect woman, he thought. In fact, he didn't, at least not right away. He cabled the factory in Harford, Connecticut, and found that they would not have another assignment for him for at least a month. He stayed at the Double M ranch for that much time.

While there, Big Thunder was allowed to wander in the pastures with some of the mares. Marilyn thought to try cross breeding the Andalusian with her paints. She wasn't sure what she'd get but according to Indian folk lore all of the breeds left by the Spaniards came from pure Andalusian horse stock. The worst she could get was a big multi colored horse that maybe could eat lightning and spit thunder. The best was something she hoped for and did not know what to expect. That didn't matter to Thunder. He just liked being what he was; a stud.

The MM cattle herds were to grow much larger giving Rocky Mountain and Abraham a future forever. They were both content with their fates to be surrounded by love and respect. What more can men ask for? The money was good, too, and Marilyn deeded them acreage every year as their retirement program. It was a good arrangement for everyone.

The town prospered, but Buck Krupp moved on. He sold off pieces of the ranch until it was divided up. No one wanted to maintain the huge old scary house so that parcel was retained by the family with enough acreage around it to maybe someday entice another Krupp heir to try living in America once again. Buck's brother stayed in prison for most of his life, while Buck was called back to Germany to help manage the weapons business. Europe was modernizing, including its weapons, and he was needed to help oversee the expansion of arms for the German military. Times were going to be good for the Krupp family of arms and he hoped he could forget his personal shame acquired in Sage Brush, Colorado.

Jedidiah Johnson and Dude Magee parted ways when in their early twenties. Their reputations as great shooters did not attract any challengers other than in competitions. Sage Brush was a pretty docile town all-in-all, so there were no real incidents. They each kept their prize matching pistols and carried them frequently. Jedidiah did become marshal of a town nearby for a while and Dude joined the Arizona Rangers and earned quite a reputation. They would meet up again some years later and their matching pistols would make for legend. But that's another story.

When Winston mounted Big Thunder to leave the Double M, Marilyn and Rocky were standing on the exact porch where they had first all encountered. Marilyn had a tear in her eye and Rocky had his arm around her shoulders.

"Rocky," Winston said, as he felt a small choke in his throat, "she's a lucky lady to have you watching over her. I've never seen you without a shirt on, but I'd be willing to bet you have two wings on your back."

"Winston," Rocky laughed, "if the good Lord wills it, maybe someday. And I expect that some years after I'm gone, you will be joining me."

"You're never gonna go, you big mountain," Marilyn said through tears streaming down her cheeks.

"I think you've got your orders, there Rocky," Winston smiled, "and Marilyn, I know I've said everything I can say, but I'll miss you. I'll be back."

"Any time, Mr. Colt. Any ol' time you feel like it," she replied sincerely.

Winston smiled and nudged Thunder to turn. He tipped his Panama hat at Marilyn and felt his heart pound. He felt different this time. He somehow sensed that leaving meant he was leaving a part of himself with her. The feeling was foreign to him. Thunder saw some of the mares he knew come to the fence they were riding past. He raised his head and whinnied deep and loudly, then he jumped but was caught by the vigilant Winston who was awakened from his potential remorse for leaving, and he reactively ordered, "Whoa Big Thunder!"

In earshot of Marilyn and Rocky they heard the order and turned to each other and laughed. Winston saw their reaction and tipped his hat again and smiled at them.

"Are you going to miss those gals?" Winston asked Thunder.

Big Thunder high stepped his way down the road.

"I guess not, eh. Oh, I see, there's always another mare in another pasture, and..." he hesitated, "but maybe not for me this time old buddy." He turned to take one last look, but Marilyn and Rocky had gone inside.

Marilyn staggered with assistance from Rocky to the settee in the living room. She looked to the high log ceiling and felt her stomach to try to ease the pain.

"Drink this water, Miss Marilyn," Rocky offered, lifting her head.

"Thanks, Rocky. I feel fine now. Must be something I ate yesterday. I feel a little different, too. Had a kind of sickness this morning when I awoke. Body's timing is off. But I'll be alright. Life is good isn't it, Rocky?"

"Ambrosia had that feeling once, just before she found out she was with..." Rocky stopped.

"Before Abraham, was what you were going to say, right?"

"Yes, Marilyn, life is good," he answered. A small tear welled in each of his eyes caused by his concern. "You're a fine person, ma'am, and life will always be good for you."